Penguin Books
Valparaiso

Penguin Books Ltd, Harmondsworth,
Middlesex, England
Penguin Books Australia Ltd, Ringwood,
Victoria, Australia

First published by Victor Gollancz 1964
Published in Penguin Books 1971
Copyright © Nicolas Freeling, 1964

Made and printed in Great Britain by
Richard Clay (The Chaucer Press) Ltd,
Bungay, Suffolk
Set in Linotype Times

Nicolas Freeling was ⸱⸱⸱
spent his childhood in ⸱⸱⸱
he worked for many y⸱⸱⸱
from their back doors ⸱⸱⸱
Europe. When *Love in Amsterdam,* his first novel, was
published in 1962 he stopped cooking other people's
dinners and went back to Holland. He now lives with
his Dutch wife and four sons in Strasbourg, between the
geese and the storks. His second and third novels,
Because of the Cats and *Gun Before Butter,* were
published in 1963. They have all been published in
Penguins, as well as *The Dresden Green, The King of the
Rainy Country, This is the Castle, Criminal Conversation*
and *Tsing Boum.* He has also written a straight novel
under a pseudonym. His latest book is *Over the High
Side* (1971).

Nicolas Freeling

Valparaiso

Penguin Books

Chapter One

'Capitaine!'

One could not have found a word better suited to carry a voice across water. Like three quick shots, followed instantly by their echo, the word floated through the still air, across the mouth of Porquerolles harbour.

From the jetty, where Christophe was standing, sloppy in a blue jumper, canvas trousers, and woolly bedroom slippers, one looked straight over westwards towards Toulon. It is only three kilometres to the big mass of pine-covered rock that forms the presqu'île – the almost-island – of Giens, across the still water of the Petite Passe. But wrapped in haze, Giens had retreated, seeming to have shrunk back for protection under the high scarp of Super-Toulon, twenty kilometres away. The whole French mainland had taken on an unreal, never-never look. Reality, one would say, was here, in the little peaceful pool of harbour.

Yet the stranger who stands on the high rocks of Giens, with nothing behind him but the flat narrow neck of land running back towards Hyères, sees Porquerolles in front of him like a golden dream and a promise. It looks romantic. It is simply another irregular mass of rock, covered like all the others in pine-trees, but it is still the Golden Isle as well as the most southerly piece of French soil there is. The name is not altogether fanciful: the reddish rock is mica-schist, very ancient, and has a golden reflection.

But the Golden Isle.... And if the stranger has read Joseph Conrad's last book – *The Rover* – and knows that he is standing, here on Giens, where Master Gunner Peyrol often stood, watching the movement of the frigate *Amelia* in the Passe – why, perhaps he can be forgiven for finding Porquerolles a romantic place.

5

Though in reality it is not romantic at all.

'Capitaine!' Christophe called again. What was there in his voice that had a tinge of something like irony? Even on a little yacht that is no more than a converted fishing boat, barely eleven metres long, there is a captain.

It was a play, perhaps, on the word. *Olivia*'s owner came, like his boat, from the north. His name was Kapitan, Raymond Kapitan, and whether a Frenchman addressed him formally, as *Olivia*'s skipper, or whether he used Raymond's name, it came to the same thing.

It is a tiny harbour, a horseshoe a couple of hundred yards across, the open, seaward side protected by a stone jetty. At the landward side, a 'hard' where boats are hauled out, and the roofs of the village behind a strip of beach. Beyond the village the pines run down to the water's edge, with here and there a villa – one of these highly ludicrous, in oriental pattern, with a minaret. The life of the harbour is concentrated on the hard and along the jetty.

Indeed the jetty shows one the whole existence of Porquerolles, arranged in neat strata. At their wooden landing-stage, *Sparrowhawk* and *Red Coral* – big decked-over launches, running the freight and passenger ferries from Giens. Then smaller launches, for private hire. Then twenty-odd fishing boats, open and simple, only seven or eight metres long. They have little motors, and even one man is enough to handle the nets and the boat. It is not a serious fishery, and can only just make a man's living.

They are pretty, these boats, with a high raked stem and narrowing to the stern-post; well suited to the short choppy waves of the coast.

There is a landing-craft, too, belonging to the Navy; ugly thing like a square metal box. And there is space for visiting yachts, which moor at the end of the jetty, where there is a little metal tower, painted red, with a flashing red light at night.

Later in the season – it was only April now – there would be yachts at anchor dotted all over the harbour, and even bigger ones outside in the Passe. Expensive yachts, with Chriscraft tenders, and brass winking in the sun. Now, in the whole harbour, there was only *Olivia*, moored the other side of the entrance, a hundred yards off the jetty, looking very prim and northern.

Not that she looked out of place; wherever there was sea-water, she would be at home. But she was quite unlike the fishing boats. A seaman would know that she really belonged over on the Atlantic coasts, among the long swinging rollers and twenty-foot tides of Finisterre. In the tideless water and short chopping seas of the Mediterranean she would always be a foreigner. Beamy and stubby, with a dead-straight stem, and a wide, square stern with a transom. In her faded black paint she was a granny. Paler and less wrinkled, fatter and less active than Provençal grannies. But a matriarch, immensely tough and solid, who has been there, making the daily soup, since living memory.

The second time that Christophe called, Raymond trotted up the first two steps of the companion, screwing up his eyes. Although there was a green sailcloth awning rigged over the afterdeck, and he was in shadow, the sun on the water, even the sun of eight in the morning in April, was hot and glaring. But there was no mistaking Christophe's silhouette, in the canvas cap pushed right back, there by the little lighthouse.

'Ho.'

'Ho.'

They exchanged a little flip of the hand, doing duty for the morning handshake across the water.

'What mosquito's biting you?'

'None. Rienco,' with a gust of laughter, Christophe's irrepressible bubble of gaiety. 'Only that if you want to haul the boat out this morning, I'll give you a hand.'

'We'll need more than two. You don't know how heavy she is.'

'The Hippocampo will help. And there is Henri.'

'Good. In half an hour? You'll be in the Escale?'

'Pardi.'

'Understood.'

Raymond dropped back into the cabin and dipped his towel carefully into the water. Fresh water is gold on a boat, but he could not stand the intensely salt water of the Mediterranean, not to wash with. Fresh water was one of his luxuries; it cost money. Even in Porquerolles, only the sun comes up for nothing.

He thought about the technical problem of getting *Olivia* out of the water. She was a deceptive boat. Looking at her across the water, from where Christophe was strolling idly back along the jetty, stopping to gossip with the Navy boys, she looked like nothing much. One saw her thirty-three feet of length and her three feet of freeboard; one did not guess that she was six feet deep, that Raymond, who was tall, could easily stand upright in her cabin. That is rare in a boat this size; she was not only a good sea-boat, but a good living-boat as well. She had been built for the deep Atlantic, at the turn of the century, and everything in her was immensely solid, very strong. She weighed eight tons; it would be hard labour to haul her with the hand-powered crane used to beach the fishing boats. We'll have to fetch her up the slipway on rollers, thought Raymond.

He was ready; it had only been a matter of tidying a few loose objects. They would haul *Olivia* out, set her with her keel on a cradle, shored up with a few planks, and give her hull the yearly treatment – a good scrub and a double coat of protective 'antifouling' paint under the waterline. It was a job for which a boatyard charged high prices; with Christophe to help, he would do it alone, for no more than the price of the paint and a few drinks, and that was most important.

He started the motor, swinging it by hand to save the batteries, slipped his mooring – a double anchor on a chain, its end tied to a cord, with an old oilcan as buoy – and, standing casually with one foot on the tiller, put the throttle on low and the engine lever ahead. The diesel thudded peacefully; *Olivia* slid in towards the hard and Raymond waved to Marius, who was just taking *Sparrowhawk* out over to Giens for the morning mail and the tourists.

Over the last fifty yards he cut the motor back to neutral; the boat carried her way, slow, ponderous, sure, up to the tiny quay; half a dozen idle turns of the propeller in reverse left her again immobile. He slung a rope fender between her side and the wall, threw a clove hitch with a light warp over an iron ring, and walked up towards the Escale, the café on the corner, for a glass with Christophe, who would be sitting there, gay and garrulous, waiting for him.

Where the wall of the café faced the harbour, under a ragged acacia, an old, crippled man in tatters and burst bedroom slippers was sitting peacefully on his heels in the dust. The deep Indian colour of his face compared painfully with white skin over bony ribs, showing through the torn shirt.

'Morning, Captain,' he said happily, with his sarcastic grin, that was due perhaps to his broken foot.

'Morning,' said Raymond rather curtly. He never much cared for that grin.

As he turned into the street facing the café – the only street in Porquerolles – he met Captain José with his white cap and big belly, his solid face as immovable, and inscrutable, as always. Raymond thought he would get it in first, this time.

'Morning, Captain.'

José slewed an eye towards him.

'Why, good day, Capitaine,' pleasantly.

Damn the bloody pack of them.

Why did they all have that identical intonation, speaking to him? Always pleasant, always polite, but always that tiny tinge of ironic amusement.

In Christophe, he could forgive it. Christophe looked at everything with irony and amusement. And Christophe was an important man, one of the island notables, a crafty and intelligent man, with some money and possessions. Syndic too of the fishermen over twenty years.

But the Hippocampo, a lightweight boy of twenty-five. Or Titi, who was scared of the sea and admitted it. Or bald, wall-eyed Giorgio the greengrocer, a cabbage-monger. Or Charley the postman.

Damn it, they did it too.

He stood a moment looking over the square, from the row of shops and little hotel-restaurants at the bottom to the church and the post-office at the top. Bare, dusty, a plane-tree here and there for much-needed shade. Nobody playing pétanque at this time of day. Instead Giorgio with his fruit stall, a few dogs scratching lazily, a couple of old women gossiping on the bench, and old Papa Tatin selling straw hats and espadrilles in his tent. Waddling across, slow and shaky, old Grand-papa Morin, in trousers too big for him, a threadbare grey cardigan, and a Basque beret – and bedroom slippers of course. Blanched, senile face. Looking like three-ha'pennyworth of nothing at all, and probably the richest man on the island. It was hot and glaring, and a dusty haze was swimming over the whole square, dancing above the cement patches.

In the café it was pleasantly cool and quiet. Christophe was hanging over the bar inside, the faded canvas cap pushed right back, black curls invading the forehead. The pale green eyes, with scarcely any brown in them, crinkled at Raymond.

'Alors. Raconte.' It was Christophe's phrase. Tell stories. He was a connoisseur of stories; nobody on the island could tell a story as he could.

'No stories. *Olivia*'s tied up to the wall.'

As always when Christophe worked, there would be a tremendous amount of walking about and talk first, gathering courage, getting bits of rope fixed, collecting wood for rollers, lively discussion over the best way to go about it all, before they spat on their fingers, promised themselves an apéritif directly the boat was out of the water, and began to heave.

There was an animated scene, with noisy advice and criticism and a good deal of cursing, that attracted onlookers – who were drawn semi-willingly into helping. The Hippocampo, young and silent, in a tartan shirt, a knitted cap, and long seaboots, with mind as well as muscle, both very useful, helped most. At last *Olivia* sat on the cradle, dripping peacefully, a good deal of weed on her propeller and rudder-mounting. They were all hot and sticky. Everybody went to the Escale for a glass, which became two. When he got back to the boat there was only Christophe, who had promised to help paint, with him. In the hot sun the woodwork, that had been a year submerged, was drying patchily. On the shadowed side little pools had formed on the cement. Raymond ducked under the bulge of the beam, opened his knife, and scraped at the slimy, weed-matted surface.

'Last year's paint still looking sound enough. But it was time she was hauled.'

Christophe's fist banged irreverently on the plank beside him.

'Solid old boat – built by somebody who knew how. What age is she now?'

'Built in eighteen ninety-nine. Count.'

'Original wood, all this?'

'Sure. Look at the thickness. You should see her frames, inside. Natural apple crooks, the way they grew.'

Christophe looked closely, stooping forward. He hunkered down, twisting his body backward and round to get close to the planks above the keel.

'What's the ballast?'

'Iron in concrete. Was lead; I think that crafty bastard in Portugal had it. Think what that amount of lead would have been worth.'

'She need a lot of pumping?'

'Ach, she makes a bit of water, not much. These old boats always do. I wring her out every ten days or so.'

'Mm.'

Christophe opened his own knife with deliberation, chose a spot just above him, and shoved the blade lightly into the wood. It sank in, with an ease and suddenness that startled Raymond. The big brown hand – loose and wrinkled looking, like an old leather glove – slapped the plank lightly, tried it with a thumbnail like a shovel, and drew out the knife delicately. A thin stream of water followed, like blood from a wound.

In a panic Raymond wriggled under a balk of paint-blotched old timber and tried his own knife, farther along. He struck again and again, as though extorting vengeance from the treacherous slimy curves of plank, so solid-looking, so beautifully shaped. But his knife met the close-grained resistance of old sea-cured hardwood; the point scarcely penetrated.

'But merciful madonna...' Christophe had made a series of careful cuts, like a seamstress pinning material to a paper pattern. Water was still trickling silently, dripping off the keel on to the sun-dried concrete.

'Hm,' said Christophe again. 'Seems about a metre long.'

'And how wide?' Raymond wanted a drink very badly indeed.

'Maybe forty centimetres. Bit big, for a piece of cheese.'

'Is all that rotted?'

'Pure camembert.'

'Let's try the other side.'

Everywhere else, the wood was solid.

Christophe stood up with a sigh, shutting his knife on his trousers after wiping the blade casually. It left a little green slime from weed. The new patch of water was already drying.

'Sixty years and more,' with regret.

'But . . . peuchère, that wood's good for over a hundred. If timberworm doesn't get it.'

'Pardi.'

'Then how . . . ?'

'Who knows? She ever been patched?'

Suddenly Raymond realized that there was a hole in his memory. It yawned precipitously before him, giving him vertigo.

'Yes, once. First year I had her. I bumped on a sandbank, and strained a couple of planks, not badly. Had her hauled just in case. Planks were all right, but the boatyard people said with an old boat it would be on the safe side to pour a bit of concrete in. But that couldn't rot the wood – damn it, it's done all the time.'

Christophe sighed heavily, staring out to sea, pushing back his hat and scratching thoughtfully.

'Who knows?' he said again. 'But I've seen things of the sort before. Maybe when they poured in the concrete they didn't line it quite close enough. Left a bubble, sealed in. Might start a moist mould, rot the whole patch from inside... You know the Artichoke!' suddenly. 'Owns the big boat from Saint-Raph? Her whole bottom's like that. He's just got himself in debt too, putting in a new motor. I told him to tow a dinghy handy, and have his knife ready to cut the painter – so...' The big hand made a sudden chopping arc through the air, sinister and expressive. 'Let's go and drink the apéritif.'

'Is that what you're telling me?'

Silence, wooden.

*

'Salut, Madame Simone. What a lovely complexion – must be good news from the bank.'

'Good morning, workers.' A stocky woman, with a bush of greying blonde hair, was holding a heavy jaw slightly sideways as she carefully added a drop of syrup to a glass.

'Two elegant pastis – like only you know how to make.'

'Yes, I know, Madame,' said Raymond as she raised her eye and stuck her lower lip out meaningly. 'I owe you twenty-five francs. I'll just have to ask you to forgive me till the end of the week.'

'Oh that's all right. I know I can rely on you.' She was already at the other end of the bar and Christophe was kicking him. But it was true: he never allowed himself to get into debt. Not that one ever could, with her.

Christophe would not talk here, either. It was as well. Apéritif time; the bar was filling up with all the regular brigade. Marius, old Léon, Charley the postman. Two pastis. Three pastis. Ice-blocks and gossip tinkled in contented partnership.

Have your knife ready to cut the painter. Or was it just one of Christophe's dramas? Idiot that he was. Not for bumping *Olivia*; that could have happened to anybody. And he had experienced her tremendous strength; she had gone on grinding there for an hour and a half under a fresh southwesterly before the tide floated her over at last. But for having stayed sitting in a café – as he was doing now – instead of watching that the workmen did the job scrupulously. A strained plank. Put on very hot tar, and then pour good cement straight on top. It had been his fault. He had sat drinking pastis.

He had a ludicrous desire to get up and run, to stay with his boat, to hold fast to the only bond with any real meaning.

Idiot. He stayed quiet and kept his voice level under the eyes of half Porquerolles.

'Found a customer for that old wreck of yours yet, Christophe?'

'*La Pupuce*? Ah no, that's my son's boat, can't sell that.'

'And supposing some maniac offered you half a million?'

'Ah, that would be different. That would be good business for my son.'

A wonderful smell was drifting out behind them from the kitchen. A waitress was laying the terrace tables with bright lobster-red cloths and napkins. Roast leg of lamb today, with garlic and rosemary. He would warm up yesterday's fish stew. It wasn't bad, but it would taste bad, because of Madame Simone's twenty-five miserable lousy francs ...

The stiff, heavy antifouling paint had to be dragged on: tiring work.

'I could find you some good wood. Ten years old. Autumn-cut.' Christophe spoke suddenly in a neutral voice.

'Oh yes, it could be done. Chip out that stinking concrete. Need a whole new bottom, pretty near. Would need very careful work to marry the new wood; have to pour in fresh concrete after. What wouldn't it cost?'

'That worry you?'

'For Christ's sake Christophe. You know I haven't a cent.'

'Well, when she's painted just put her back in the water. She's all right in harbour. All right to go to Toulon in, except maybe in the mistral. Why worry? Bloody Artichoke's out every day in his, and his is ten times worse than yours.'

'To go to Toulon – not quite the same as South America.'

Valparaiso, he thought. Failing that, nothing was any good.

Chapter Two

It cheered him, though, to climb back on his boat. It always did. He was tired, but with an honest job well done. Not quite honest – they had painted over a gangrene. Christophe had found some sheet tin, fiddled out of the Navy doubtless, in some mysterious manner. They had painted over the patch, tacked the tin over with copper nails, well stretched, and painted again over that. But the patch was still there.

Raymond lay, very tired, on the left-hand cabin bunk, and patted the leather with his open hand. Leather that had been there over sixty years. Scratched, rubbed, shiny, cracked, scarred, stained. All *Olivia*'s history was written in that leather.

She had been built in England, as a fishing boat. Called, vaguely, a 'Looe lugger'. Just an open boat, with the simplest possible rig, half decked, with nothing aft but a tangle of fishermen's rubbish. Why are fishermen the dirtiest and sloppiest of all boat-handlers? But they can build.

Probably she hadn't even had a name, but just a number. She had earned her bread out in the Atlantic, with pilchards or whatever. Then, perhaps between nineteen ten and fourteen, when sailing became first respectable, then a passion, for rich men, she had been bought and converted to a yacht. It had been a heroic period. Captain McMullen with his little boats that all had heroic, star-dusted names. *Perseus, Orion*. He had written *Down Channel*, the first classic of single-handed amateur sailing for the pleasure of it. There had been Childers too – *The Riddle of the Sands*. Looming up over the horizon had been Doctor Claud Worth, Moses of yachtsmen.

The boat had been bought by someone like that, and converted to a gaff cutter, with a sailroom where the engine now was, between the cabin and the cockpit. The cutter rig and the simple, heavy gear suited her perfectly. Now, it looked ludicrously old-fashioned, when cutters are all slim elegant Bermudas, but Raymond had never cared. He knew that he had the best of all rigs, and the only one that can be managed single-handed. Not fast, but efficient, economical, safe, and surprisingly powerful.

A single stumpy mast, and a boom like a telegraph pole. No topmast. Her 'plain' sail was just a main, a staysail with the sheet on a horse, and a big jib on the lowslung bowsprit. There were no complications whatever; a minimum of ropes and blocks. If he had had spinnakers or square-sails, he would not have known what to do with them.

In shallow water, with a light wind, of course, sailing was very leisurely, and with her unusual depth *Olivia* would have been a cow to wriggle into the harbours of the Channel or the North Sea. Awkward harbours, with mudbanks everywhere and tremendous tides. Nobody had any use for motors, then. He could just picture the original owner, whiskered, in check knickerbockers (and perhaps the original Olivia, whaleboned but sportive, with a dear little hat), kedging off those mudbanks.

But by the thirties women wore trousers, and no longer enjoyed the spartan pleasures of kedging off. (When stuck in the mud, you row off in the dinghy, and drop an anchor on a long warp. By heaving on this anchor, you may get the yacht off the mud. Mostly, the anchor comes. Either way, the operator gets covered in mud.) *Olivia*'s owner had put in a motor, and it was this motor, Raymond declared proudly, that made her the finest boat of her size afloat. It was a flat twin-cylinder diesel, laborious to start but absolutely reliable, and willing to push *Olivia*'s solid bulk at five knots in slack water all day and night. It disregarded any quantity of salt water, never needed attention, and always ran on the first swing. Small marine engines that are not incurable whores are the greatest rarity afloat. This motor had saved Raymond's life as well as a great deal of breath, skin, blood, and sickening fear.

It had a dynamo, charged two twelve-volt accumulators, and gave the boat electric light throughout. It could power a radio transmitter, but Raymond was not that kind of sailor. He also preferred oil-lamps, except in emergencies and for the navigation lights, when sailing at night.

It had all been the purest chance. He might easily have found a French boat, prettier, with finer lines, a better sailer. But not as comfortable, as roomy, as reliable. He had fallen in love with *Olivia* at sight, and never regretted her.

She was admirably fitted inside, too, like a pre-1914 Russian railway carriage. Everything was teak, except a rococo cast-iron stove, and a brass rail round it to stop pots falling off in a sea-way. The oven served admirably to keep food cool. The folding table was a solid slab of teak, that nothing could scratch, and the bulkheads would have resisted an elephant.

The leather-covered settees in the cabin slept two. There was a sleeping cabin forward, but Raymond had abolished it; on one side all his sails were stored, and on the other winter clothes, oilskins, boots. The lavatory was forward of this, in the bows, next to the chain locker. In the engine room he kept paint, wire, tools, and screws. Diesel oil went into a tank at the back of the cockpit. This cockpit was no more than an oblong slit in the deck, with the tiller, the very simple engine controls, and on either side the fore- and main-sheets, coiled on bitts. In front of the tiller was the binnacle. There were lockers in the cockpit for instruments, but he had few. He had no radio or searchlight, no depth meter or sonar. He had a bearing compass and two big torches, a few flares and the first-aid box, a leadline and a patent log; a spare knife, a pair of pliers, some lengths of rope and wire. Everything large and simple. The binnacle, its ancient compass rose marked with rusty stains, was indeed brass, but he had never polished it and wasn't going to begin, either.

Really essential equipment was in the saloon. Here he had a sextant, and two pairs of binoculars – one for night work. A chronometer – utterly sacred, wound every morning before drinking coffee – and barometer, and a tell-tale compass. He had his charts, in two huge shallow drawers under the bunks, and his working books; star-sight and tide tables, the nautical almanac, pilots for all the European coasts. Doctor Worth on yacht maintenance, and the engine handbook.

The saloon was his great pride. He always kept it clean and

tidy, and rubbed the woodwork with linseed oil. It had lockers above and below the bunks, and bookshelves on all the bulkheads. On one side of the companion – the little set of steps to the deck, with a sliding roof and a tiny pair of folding doors – was a little sink and a draining board, and Raymond's toothbrush, and on the other was a zinc-lined locker for food. There were fresh-water tanks on both sides, behind, and the sink had a salt-water tap with a pump. The stove was forward, against the sailroom bulkhead; Raymond had taken out the antique grate and put in a Buta cylinder. He had a two-burner here, and a single-burner with a gas cartridge in the cockpit, to heat dinner on a passage. The cabin was lit by three old-fashioned brass paraffin lamps in gimbals, and every movable object was secured against rolling. The gas stoves were in gimbals too, and the bookshelves had slats at the front, so that books could not fall out.

A lot of Raymond's books were the sailing classics – Captain Voss and Joshua Slocum beside Worth and McMullen, Alain Gerbault and the voyages of the discoverers. The rest were his own discoveries – odd volumes of Conrad beside things like *The Story of San Michele* and *The Great White South*. Unless one counted the Conrads, there wasn't any literature. Nearly everything had been bought on sixpenny stalls in the first place, and all had been read and reread, generally while eating, till the coffee-stained, oil-smeared pages, many sprinkled with sea-water, were falling out of the faded bindings. It was a solitary person's library – Dumas next to Bougainville, and Dumont d'Urville, rather surprised, up against snappy stories with rather good pornographic illustrations.

Raymond was a good sailor. He could not talk jargon: he called port and starboard left and right. He knew nothing of the affected etiquette of ensigns and pennants, and despised varnish and brass-polish as he did Bermuda rig. But he could take a good star sight – it is not easy from the deck of a small boat – and he knew every light and landmark from Ushant to Corsica. He could sail and steer his boat anywhere, in any weather, given plenty of sea room. He had awkward fingers, but had taught himself, painfully, the ways of wind and water.

18

He knew he was a good enough sailor to cross the Atlantic. He certainly had a good enough boat.

Here, in the Mediterranean, everything was easy. No tide, or tide currents. No damp, and little rain or mist, that in the north meant endless work with sandpaper and steel wool, paint and vaseline. In a good harbour, like this one, there was only the heat as enemy: the sun that opened deck seams and the cabin roof, that could snap a wire shroud like a carrot, and make the binnacle hot enough to raise a blister. He had nailed canvas over the deck, and fixed an awning over the cabin and cockpit. And *Olivia*, with her low freeboard and thick wooden planks, was a cool boat. Not like a modern steel ketch, or a fibre-glass motor-boat – one would be forced to spend all day ashore, with one of those things.

If there was still any water to leak out the paint had stopped it. They had left *Olivia* on the improvised stocks, shored up with a careless-looking plank on either side, wedged home with empty oildrums. She would stay stranded on the dusty concrete – dabbled now with rust coloured splashes of paint – until tomorrow, when she would get a second coat. Christophe had worked hard – and for nothing, for friendship. Or rather, perhaps, comradeship. It was not out of pity. Christophe was not that kind of person. These people are not sentimental. None of them, ever. They leave that to northerners, like Raymond.

Wasn't that why he liked them? No pretences, and no misty idealisms, and, if they were dishonest, it was not to themselves. They looked at life, and made neither complaints nor excuses. Mm, he wished he could say the same.

Was a boat not a pathetic object, like this, out of the water, propped up insecurely with a dirty plank and a rusty oildrum? At the mercy of any drunk that cared to piss against her. He felt himself as awkward and helpless – even to climb on to her deck he had to scramble foolishly up a ladder, worried lest he might be sniggered at by the village children.

As the tourists came straggling past, towards the six o'clock boat back to the mainland, they stared stupidly, he thought, with mean little peasant eyes, full of envy and hostility. He owned a boat, and was therefore, doubtless, a stinking capitalist. It was infuriating to think that any one of these noisy factory workers, with a wife and a rented flat and three snivelling brats, should have three times the money he had.

Her hull is rotten, he told himself. To repeat it, meaninglessly, gave him a sort of obscure pleasure, like prodding at the gum of a sore tooth. By adding an extra pain, one imagined that the first diminished. And that was all that he could do. To hold on, clinging with his eyes shut, until it lessened. He did not fight back; what was the good when one could never win? He accepted; meek, passive, fatalistic; he had accepted many other defeats the same way. He had perhaps learned better how to take a punch, that was all. He shrugged; he accepted.

He looked at his larder; the world wagged on and he still got hungry. At the weekend, he would buy some meat, but for today, again, he had had yesterday's fish, and for tomorrow there would be today's fish – he hoped. He would take the dinghy out to Notre Dame, and sink a little net. If nobody else had picked the same place, off the fort, that Christophe had told him would be a good one in this weather.

After eating – soup made with fish heads, with a few odd vegetables and plenty of rice, garlic, and saffron, very economical – he had a cigarette. Tobacco was precious – he allowed himself ten a day and generally managed to keep to it. Ach, he was depressed, that was all. It was bad, too, to sleep on land, he who always slept on water, ready to slip off, with nobody else's snoring to listen to. And he was tired – the painting had been mortal hard work. He was no longer twenty – and he hadn't Christophe's sea-hardened toughness, more's the pity, though he was wiry enough.

It was a wonderful night; the frogs were quacking like mad up the hill from the harbour, by the Navy barracks. He would just smoke his cigarette, and then get out and let his net have a few hours nightfall down there where the fish would be strolling about. The soup had been good. Oh, he knew how to be patient, and sparing. He even knew how to let tobacco take the place of food, if necessary, for many, many hours if need be. He wasn't going to be able to sail the Atlantic single-handed, right down into the icy south, through the storms, round the

Horn to Valparaiso, without being able to suffer some hard-ship. And as for *Olivia*'s hull, might it perhaps be a question – he was leaning on the oars of the dinghy, half-way along the coast towards the Point of Notre Dame – that the Corse would be able to answer?

Chapter Three

Raymond was born, grew up, and till he was past twenty never left, one of those towns that are not capitals, and always remain invincibly provincial, but are the administrative centre of an area and have great local importance. In recent times, they have converted the most impressive of their buildings into bureaucratic beehives, surrounded their outskirts with concrete blocks, modernized their shopping centres round a formerly pretty square, and then sat back, well pleased with themselves and their municipal enterprise. Bordeaux or The Hague, Stuttgart or Antwerp. These towns have often many beautiful buildings from the seventeenth and eighteenth centuries, having enjoyed much commercial importance in their time, and have generally a palace, built by a reigning duke or some minor royalty. They will also have a town hall and a palace of justice, both rather grand. There will certainly be ponderous and sometimes black buildings of the nineteenth century, and a fine row of banks, insurance companies, and local industrial tyrants with big breeches.

They have anything up to a million inhabitants, three or four large hotels, and a dozen or so chain stores like huge phosphorescent slugs. These all look exactly the same, and whether they are called Kaufhof or Innovation or Lafayette or C. and A. the merchandise they sell is identical. One can only tell the country by looking to see which language the no smoking signs are printed in.

But increasingly these towns tend to look more and more like one another. A business man from Japan or Nigeria, looking out of his hotel window at the street and the trams and the ants, finds it more and more difficult to say which country he has arrived in now. The intellectual poverty of these provincial towns becomes more and more pronounced as they become more and more municipalized, hygienic, progressive, and bourgeois.

It was the grandest of the hotels, facing the little park, with the most expensive and exclusive shops on either side of it, that had fascinated Raymond all his childhood, and had become a symbol of achievement, something that he must reach. It was called the Hôtel des Indes, probably to recall a time everybody had forgotten, when the town had been a pioneer in the trade with the Indies. The pavement here was broad, and the lamp-posts sat upon painted cast-iron lions, that supported on the one side shields with the city arms, and on the other side ornate litter-baskets. Beggars anywhere on this stately pavement were shooed by officious policemen in high boots, and trams were only allowed to go clinking and sparking round the other three sides.

Opposite the hotel taxis were lined up, 'under the railings' as people still called it, though the graceful wrought-iron work that had surrounded the lindens had been given away in a flush of patriotism, to make tanks in Adolf's time. A gigantic porter in a yellow top-hat used to stand on the top step of the hotel entrance and blow on a little silver whistle to summon those taxis. Now that it was 1948, he was again doing it, with an artificial foot that added lustre to the traditional performance.

New curtains, too, hung now at all the windows of the Hôtel des Indes, the dangerously rusted little balconies had been repaired, and though trees had been cut down all over the town in the hunger winter, the lindens still spread their green carpet opposite. The façade, repainted in the original yellow ochre, now showed hardly any of the scars – an over-enthusiastic resistance worker with three hand-grenades, for in Adolf's time 'Des Indes' had been requisitioned by an Oberkommando.

There was a new American bar now, the kitchens had been modernized, and this very year, the local newspaper had announced proudly, there were no less than seventy-three new private bathrooms, where important industrial individuals could pull the plug without, for once, inviting publicity.

Raymond did not know why he was so fascinated by that stretch of pavement. He had never set foot in any of the shops and had never even stayed in a hotel – indeed the one family connection was his father's turn-out at the annual dinner of the Law Society, and that was held in Hôtel Terminus, which was dingier and more anonymous, altogether less grand, in a downtrodden business quarter by the station, where all the windows belonged to manufacturers' wholesalers and displayed ball-bearings.

Since he had been eighteen, in his last year at the lyceum, with his first adult suit, he had taken an assiduous walk, daily, along that stretch of sacred pavement. The windows had been boarded up then, and he had had to rely on the extravagant nostalgia of his childhood memories. But now that the high life had returned, he was determined to enter it, and he studied the fur-coated women going into the hairdresser, stockbrokers on their way to lunch at the University Club, and the underfed pageboys who held umbrellas on rainy days, all with the same passion.

Officially he was a student still – Arts, third year – but he had not been to a lecture in months. To his friends and to his dubious but fascinated mother he boasted that he was an actor. He got up at eleven, and avoided having his hair cut for as long as he possibly could, despised all churches, and frequently quoted Sartre. He certainly ran about the theatre a great deal and knew all its corners. He was a useful and alert holder of spears, gave a hand with scene-painting, had been promised a speaking part next time there was a large cast, and occasionally, after receipts had been good, was called Assistant Stage Manager and paid a pound. He was on christian-name terms with Arnold the producer, Carl the scene-designer, painter, and prop-maker, and old Thomas the doorkeeper. He had learned to kiss the hands of actresses, both real and would-be.

His father, after a year's warfare, had decided not to surrender exactly, but to take no further notice. At home, Raymond was knowledgeable about amber floats and the O.P. side and Barrault, and if the pounds were a bit irregular, just look at the experience he was getting – that was what counted.

His father was greffier – a sort of superior clerk – in the Palace of Justice. Learned in the law, possessed of a judicial-looking robe, with a little desk and an owlish look at assize sittings. His name was familiar to everyone – it was always printed at the foot of minatory legal notices in the local paper beginning 'Whereas'.

In pre-war years, of respect and the Old Order, this position had been and, better, looked an important and affluent one. In those days a briefcase under the arm, a sonorous title, a flat with comfortable furniture, and a pension at the end of devoted public service – that was something. Raymond's childhood was spent regarding himself as the shoot of a rather grand family. Imposing to make walks in a sailor suit on Sunday afternoons and see his father take his hat off for the Public Prosecutor – and see Him take His hat off.

But at the lyceum, in wartime, it had already been a disillusion to be snubbed by the sons of pork-butchers and characters with contracts for Army boots. Whereas Raymond had had to be aided by a scholarship to get to the lyceum at all. Still, he had been his father's pride when he had been runner-up, ex aequo, at the university entrance examination open to the whole province, and received the subsidy, without which, it was explained to him, it would be impossible to give him the education that was so necessary.

For after forty-five times were hard, money no longer quite real, and state legal functionaries not quite what they had been. Raymond's theatrical aura had been the first thing that brought him a little prestige among his comrades. Most of them were now in Papa's business (making great strides amidst all the Marshall Aid) and hating this bondage. He had even been a hero one day – he had knocked, trembling, on the dressing-room door of the new young star actress, who was adored by his contemporaries, to borrow a safety-pin. She was sitting in front of her glass, in a glamorous if sluttish scene of confusion, naked to the waist, and had given him the safety-pin without even taking her eyes off her cheekbone, which she was carefully painting.

It had given him enormous confidence; he had even walked into the Hôtel des Indes, and been surprised to find it all quite easy. Nobody had even really looked at him. He was quite thick by now with the bartender, whom everybody called Jim. The drinks were expensive; he generally had imported Pilsener, the cheapest thing they had.

He had had a snub though, last time. He had been hanging on a stool in the dim light, very much at home, dressed rather artistically in a high-necked sweater, when a pale archangel of an assistant manager, flitting through, had glanced at him, frowned, and had a whispered colloquy with the barman. Jim had strolled over afterwards, polishing a glass elaborately, and leaned across the bar.

'Look, kid, I've just had a telling-off from Wigwag there – I'm not to serve you unless you're properly dressed.'

Raymond was indignant.

'Yeh, I told him you were an actor but he won't have it. Collar and tie or no service.'

He had slunk out, rather.

At home, after a campaign, he had been given the money to buy a suit. They were going to do an American comedy at the theatre – he would have lines – Arnold would never allow that utility thing that was all he had – he could not jeopardize this most important chance. It worked. Well pressed – and presentable, since he was tall and narrow – he could now sit at the bar with confidence.

It was nearly empty this evening. It was too early of course, but he had to go to the theatre – he was a cadet of Gascony, in *Cyrano*, with a moustache, doctored wellington boots, and a rapier that hardly looked tarnished – and scarcely needing any false hair. Some industrial buyer was sitting quietly in a corner writing up notes, with an imitation jade cigar-holder and the statutory whisky, and at the bar there was only a girl, fidgeting with a glass of sherry.

'Hi, Jim. Usual please. Have to make it quick; due at the theatre in twenty minutes.'

Hm, pretty girl. Very long, very smooth blonde hair, parted on one side, falling over the shoulders in negligent waves, and a modish frock. She might have been twenty. She took a cigarette from a little silver case, laid it aside, and started examining an arched eyebrow in a little mirror. Was there a spot, or wasn't there a spot? Her handbag – it must have been her first – slid off her crossed knees and crashed on to the floor. Raymond, all gallantry, was over in a flash.

'Permit, Mademoiselle.'

'Oh, thank you very much.'

'Surely you're not alone?' hopeful.

'Oh no, I'm waiting for my mother, thank you.'

He couldn't think of anything to say, smiled awkwardly, and took refuge in noisy conversation.

'Ah, Jim lad, good receipts this week. *Cyrano*'s doing well, surprisingly. But Arnold's terrific of course – worth seeing just for the nose ... "Nous sommes les cadets de Gascogne",' he intoned with a sweep. Aha, the girl was reacting.

'Oh, are you in that?'

'Why yes, Mademoiselle, I'm the stage manager, but I'm playing this week – have to stalk about, y'know.'

'I'm going tonight. I hear it's fun. Oh, here's my mother.' Stout furred woman, returning from tremendous repairs in the powder room.

'Oh there you are, Pauline; what are you doing here?'

'Having a sherry.'

'Well why didn't you sit in the lounge, silly child, and have a waiter bring it? In the bar – really. Now come on, we haven't much time; I'll have one at the table.'

The girl fumbled in the bag to pay.

'No, no, Mademoiselle, my pleasure, please.'

She didn't know how to refuse, and Mamma was already outside, impatient.

'Thank you,' awkwardly.

'See you in the theatre,' said Raymond, grandiose.

And indeed, there she was, in the second row; no mistaking the hair. Raymond had a wonderful idea, a romantic idea. At the end of the fourth act, after the battle, when the cadets took a curtain call from an excited audience, he took a property rose that he had stuck in his hair, and tossed it neatly. The rose hit her in the neck; she was clapping hard. Mother, wearing horn-rimmed glasses, was scrabbling in a chocolate box and never noticed. She waved the rose happily. It was the only romantic gesture of Raymond's entire life.

'Who is it?' he had asked Jim.

'I know the mother, and the father's here often. One of these old families. Lots of money. They have a big house out in the foothills. They've horses – I don't know what all. When the father comes in here, I give him quarter-bottles of champagne with a brandy.'

Raymond was much impressed; he pumped his father.

'Oh yes. Been here since the French time.'

The local people spoke of history this way. They talked about 'the Spanish time'. The 'French time' meant Napoleon. Now of course the nasty word 'occupation' was being replaced by 'the German time'.

'Owns a lot of land, has vineyards, big shareholder in the steelworks over north of the river – very rich. Doesn't seem to have lost any either. I wonder who it'll go to – there was a son, but killed in the Air Force.'

To do Raymond justice it was the 'first families' more than the money that he fell in love with. The Hôtel des Indes, and his assiduous haunting of The Pavement, had paid off at last.

He took the bus out to where wooded hills wound up towards distant mountains, massive and rounded like the Vosges, where all the first families lived. He discovered big iron gates, stone pillars with a crest above them, a high wall overhung with dripping greenery. Of the inside he could see nothing but the edge of a lawn and the branch of a cedar. It was a rainy autumn; the foothills were full of mist.

He was out there four times on his free Sundays, and was in despair of ever seeing her again when he was suddenly pierced with thumping dry breathlessness by the sight of a horse.

The horse was a lightly built, pretty chestnut; Pauline sat it comfortably at a walk, astride, in jodhpurs, her hair tied back with a ribbon. He had no idea that she had kept the rose, and had it in the pocket of her Scotch tweed hacking jacket. It was the kind of thing she had imagined, at the convent.

He probably would not have had the courage to utter, at last, but she saw him.

'Why hallo. What are you doing out in the wilds?'

'Oh I came to have peace to study up a part. Er – do you live out this way, then?'

'I live in here,' casually, waving at the wall. 'Morbid dump it is' – a phrase that flabbergasted him.

'But you do go into the town?'

'Of course, every day. Not that there's much life there, but at least there's something besides trees.'

Raymond took his daring in his hands.

'Why don't we have coffee some morning – in the Golden Pheasant perhaps?'

'Oh yes, I like it there, I enjoy all those pictures.' It was a small restaurant combined with picture gallery, with appeal for the richer of the local intelligentsia.

'Tomorrow if you like. I've nothing particular to do.'

Pauline was just the right age for Cyrano, for Roxane, for whispers under balconies. Raymond's gaucheries and snobberies did not bother her in the slightest. She would have liked to tell him to get the gardener's ladder, and climb to her window at night, but it did not occur to her. She was no Mathilde. If she had she would have found him a great coward – he was no Julien. But she had wonderful hair, and a ringing name. Pauline Régie de Beaugency. Some younger son, with a court post under one of Napoleon's brothers – Louis, or Jerome. Pauline was a family name, borrowed from the splendid Bonaparte princess – it was whispered that an ancestor had had an affair with her.

He would always recall one ghastly humiliation. They were in the Golden Pheasant, and had eaten creamy cake. Pauline wanted an ice, one of those fancy ones, with fruit and whipped cream. He had only ten shillings in his pocket and asked for the bill trembling. Oh god, eleven and six, without the tip. Oh god ... what a supercilious, disdainful face that waiter had.

'Stupid of me, I seem to have forgotten my wallet. Have you any loose change, Pauline?'

'Not a penny, I'm afraid,' quite unconcerned.

'Oh dear ... I'll just look in the street; sure to find some friend on The Pavement. So sorry. Look, waiter ... it's embarrassing ... I'll be right back. Look, the young lady will stay

29

here, as security, you know ... I won't be two minutes.'
Ghastly, it sounded.

Pauline just sat there grinning; the waiter had those horrible
raised eyebrows. In the street he gasped; where on earth to find
a couple of bob? He thought of the tight mouth of his mother's
brother in the cigar-shop, and his heart fell into his socks. He
ran like a lunatic to the Hôtel des Indes fifty metres away, and
tried to control his sobbing breath. If Jim refused, or wasn't
there ...

'Jim lad, be a real pal and lend me five bob. I'm out with that
blonde – you know' – with a leer – 'and I've run a fraction
short. Half a crown'd do it.' He tried not to have a mendicant's
voice.

The barman jingled what seemed like five pounds' worth of
silver in his pocket.

'Why sure, kid. Here, here's ten bob. All right?'

'God, Jim, you've saved my life. Thanks, sport ...'

'Oh you're still here. So stupid of me. I saw Andreas, you
know, the tall actor – played De Guiche – friend of mine. No
trouble. Waiter ...'

Pauline always produced pound notes, afterwards. She had
plenty of money, she said indifferently. It didn't worry her that
he was poor, that his father was only the greffier at the law-
courts, that they lived in a dark old-fashioned flat in a rather
gloomy nineteenth-century house rather too near the prison.
She loved him.

But she didn't quite dare ask him to her home, and he –
what could he do, at home, with his mamma hovering, with
tea and biscuits no doubt? Oh how to see her away from
public places? The best they could do was walks ... Sometimes
they found the Botanic Gardens deserted, and kissed each
other furiously behind palm trees, not caring for the eagle eye
of a totally indifferent functionary in dark-blue uniform, busy
scrubbing the huge horrible leaves of the Victoria Regia water-
lily.

They concocted a tremendous enterprise at last; they were
being driven nearly silly. He would hire a room for the night,

in the Hôtel Terminus, where nobody knew either of them. She would say she was going to a friend's house, a girl from the convent who lived in the next town forty kilometres away, and would ring up to say she was staying the night. He would say he had scene-painting, lighting rehearsal – easy to contrive a theatre excuse for being away all night. For a dress rehearsal he was never home before four, on Monday mornings sometimes.

The room was a hateful beige colour, and the sudden mutterings, creakings, and heavy steps in the passage were terrifying. On the wall was a notice giving the times of table d'hôte meals. Guests staying later than midday will be charged an extra night. Please leave your Key at the Office. Outside the dingy net curtain was a smell of cabbage, and a cat exploring dustbins, and a loud noise of a late tram in the almost deserted street. Undressing Pauline on the lumpy bed was almost an anticlimax; neither of them was exactly expert.

But the adventure gave them a new boldness with each other, and a week later, out with the horse in a spinney on top of one of the low foothills, on a dry day for once, he urgently undid Pauline's jodhpurs. The pine needles left a pattern all over her bottom, and the horse stood by with a sniffy, disdainful expression.

He only had her four times in all. None of them really a success. The last time, she got a green smear on her frock from a laurel bough and laddered a stocking. She also got pregnant.

Raymond sweated; Pauline seemed quite undisturbed.

'We'll just get married, that's all. We'll manage; other people do. Papa will give us an allowance, since we can't live yet on your theatre work. When you're famous, nobody will think anything of it. Just don't say or do anything till you hear from me.' She would tell her father and it would all arrange itself.

'Letter for you,' said old Thomas. A long typewritten envelope, crisp as a new bank note, addressed to 'Artists' Entrance'. It didn't look very like Pauline; he palpitated.

There was a handwritten half-sheet, not sounding like her either.

31

Mr Raymond Kapitan.

You will please come to the Hôtel des Indes, on Tuesday the eleventh of this month, at ten in the morning precisely, and make your self known at the desk. We can then have a conversation that will benefit both of us.

Artur H. C. de B scribble.

He was greeted at the desk of Des Indes with a nod, and a page brought him to one of the 'conference rooms' – particularly nasty invention of up-to-date hotels. They are arranged in suites with folding partitions, so that business men can either plot piracy with two intimates, or address winged words to an audience of three-hundred hung-over salesmen. This one was reduced to its tiniest, smelt of fresh paint, was very bare, and immediately forbidding. There was nobody there; he lit a cigarette and tried to look in command of a table, two hard little chairs, and three ash-trays.

The door opened suddenly; he turned and faced hot-tempered eyes in a thin long face. Horsy clothes: a jacket like Pauline's, of expensive imported Scotch tweed, bedford cords, veldschoens, a checked flannel shirt, and a rust-coloured tie. Mr Artur de Beaugency looked like a wealthy trainer of race-horses.

He did not sit either. He walked to the ponderous chimney-piece – left in to give atmosphere after the central heating had been installed; the hearth had been filled with a panel, and the florist had arranged some inadequate sprays of left-over ever-green in a sort of crematory urn in front – and took a Colombian cigarette from a long curved case that probably matched the silver brandy-flask in his other pocket. All these details were found later engraved on Raymond's memory.

'What I have to say is quite short, perfectly simple, and needs the presence of no third person. I have just come from seeing your father, whom I know to be a man of integrity and judgement. He is in full agreement with what I have to tell you. I will admit at once that my fingers itch to give you a sound beating, but although the idea is tempting it would not arrange matters. You will not, of course, marry my daughter, nor will you see her again, nor will you stay in this town. I have taken the trouble to find out that you have nothing to do here that could be of value to anybody. You have abandoned your university studies, and the man who gives you theatrical employment tells me that he has no use for you beyond the odd errands you at present run. It is evident that if you are to make anything of your life it will be elsewhere.' He paused, looked at the three ash-trays with dislike, and flicked his ash at the evergreens.

'I considered all that. Rather strangely, I decided to help you. I will give you a substantial sum of money and I will give you the name of a firm in Lisbon, business relations of mine, who you will find will help you. If you should reappear here' – he paused to find a suitable phrase – 'you will forfeit my consideration. Have you anything to say?'

Raymond looked for things to say; he was too jolted out of his balance and his self-esteem to find anything. It was all too much to absorb at one moment.

'No – that is to say – I don't know – I have to think . . .'

The man cut him short abruptly.

'I have the cheque in my pocket.' He sat down at the table and signed his name with a rapid assured movement; the rest was already written. 'One thousand pounds. To do with – as you please.'

Raymond stood like a stuffed fish; a thin brown hand waved the fluttering paper to dry it and thrust it at him; he took it limply.

'And there is a card of mine – the address in Lisbon is on the back.' Scribbled across the face was 'You would oblige me in assisting this young man to some employment – H.C.B.' Raymond pushed this shaming thing in his pocket hastily.

'Hm,' said the man, after adding him up for a moment out of narrowed eyes – strange, they were Pauline's eyes – 'I think that I have good reason to be glad that I have acted so. Good day.' He quite simply turned and walked out, not even bothering to shut the door. That was a job for a footman after all.

Directly he was gone, leaving nothing but a faint whisper of South American tobacco, Raymond found himself capable again of uttering. He was astonished, indignant – but mostly angry at missing the opportunity. It had all gone too fast. Fellow hadn't given him a second, but had twisted his arm after distracting him with half-veiled insults. Glad he had acted so. Arnold had no use. Nothing of value to anybody. Sound beating. Forfeit consideration. By what right did the fellow talk like that?

If he had had an hour to think it out he would not have accepted either insults or cheque. He would have made a scene. 'You can't stop us – I'm twenty-two and she's twenty. She's carrying my child. No threats or promises will stop me.'

The man hadn't made any threats or promises.

Damn it, that was what had buggered him up. The man had simply made a few self-assured, half-contemptuous statements, and squashed him like a moth.

Because he was poor and had no job? Because he hadn't been able to find words fast enough? Why had the fellow said he was glad?

It was too late to do anything; he had taken the cheque and the card. A year and more later Raymond would realize – only then – that the words were a consequence of his taking the cheque and the card. In taking them, he had not only abandoned Pauline, he had sold her.

He had been reading Conrad's *Lord Jim*. When the thought struck him, he took the book and threw it overboard in a rage.

Like Lord Jim, he had jumped.

Chapter Four

There is a restaurant – and small hotel – on the island of Porquerolles that is called the Arche de Noé. It is always pleasant, but most pleasant at ten-thirty on a hot morning because a stranger, his eyes still dazzled by the sparkling water, his ears irritated by the engine of the ferry-boat and the chatter in the harbour, walks from a hot dusty square into peace. There is nobody to be seen, and the surroundings are wonderfully quiet.

As the stranger's eyes become accustomed to the different light he sees, first, an old Provençal tiled floor that has just been washed with fresh water, and dark old Provençal furniture: bars, stools, and tables, gleaming with polish. It is not dark, or even dim; it is an underwater light. There are Roman amphorae, patterned with grey and brown stains that are almost a patina. They have been for centuries under the sea. So, one can easily believe, has the dark blue seltzer siphon and the glazed earthenware water jug on the bar. Even the big bunches of myrtle and arbustes arranged in the amphorae seem to be of submarine origin; it is difficult to picture them growing in the sun.

The stranger, this particular morning, was a woman called Natalie Servaz. She was tired, nervous, and depressed, and the first impact of the Arche was a promise of oblivion. She leaned upon the bar and examined the picture behind it, above the rows of glasses and apéritif bottles.

It was an incongruous, ridiculous picture, both comic and peaceful, which is a good combination. It was very large, and vaguely Flemish-looking, representing one of those extraordinary farmyards populated with every imaginable domestic beast. What was a Flemish farmyard doing, in heaven's name, behind a bar in Porquerolles?

Turkey-cocks, geese, donkeys, peacocks, bantam-cocks, and ordinary cocks, all mixed up with dogs and sheep and masses of improbable vegetables painted in loving detail. The animals were all looking the same way with an air of theatrical self-satisfaction, like the Bremen street musicians.

Natalie enjoyed this picture very much. She slid on to one of the stools and tapped her sunglasses on the bar.

'Is there nobody?' she said. She had the clear careful voice, modulated and articulated, of an actress who may not be good but is competent.

A woman appeared from submarine depths. Really she had been sitting behind the bar, deep in accounts, but one thought of some animal poised motionless on the sea-bottom, nibbling delicately at algae. Natalie looked at her in slight surprise, though she was a perfectly ordinary woman in a northern-looking skirt and woolly.

It was pleasant to have seen and heard nothing for weeks, and then to have so sharp and immediate a picture of quiet. She needed badly to heal, and made up her mind with a decision that startled her – it seemed some time since she had made one.

'Have you a room free?'

'Certainly, Madame. For long?' The voice hovered delicately, like a rather greedy humming-bird.

'Perhaps. I don't know. Maybe a month. Maybe longer.'

'With pleasure. Next month, it may be difficult. The season, Madame understands.'

'I can always see,' impatiently. 'My name is Servaz. I will have my luggage sent. Can I telephone?'

'But naturally.'

'And give me a drink, if you will.'

'A little whisky?'

'No.' She tried to think. 'A glass of white wine.'

It was a Côtes de Provence; the bottle was covered in condensation and the label said 'Domaine de l'Aumerade–à Pierrefeu (Var)'. It was young, a little tart. Drinking it, Natalie felt she was floating effortlessly, drifting from leaf to leaf like a dandelion seed.

'I have your Paris number, Madame. Shall I branch it to the cabin?'

'I'll take it here... That you, Félicie? I'm in the Midi, on an island called Porquerolles, got that? Pack me a couple of cases, would you – no, nothing elaborate, no town stuff. Beach things, and what I'll need for a month or so. Send it to a hotel called Noah's Ark... Félicie, tell Monsieur, will you? ... Yes, yes, just that I'm resting, that's all. I'm perfectly all right. Give him my love; tell him I'll ring him, or write him, or something, and not to be the least anxious. Have you understood? ... Good, right, I can count on you – no no, I'm fine. Bye.'

'I will get someone to show Madame her room.'

'My luggage will be here tomorrow.'

'We will see that it is safely brought.'

'I'm going for a stroll. Back by one anyway.'

'When you please. Enjoy your walk.'

'Thank you,' said Natalie.

It was an effort to force herself out into the humming sunlight; her legs felt unsteady. Unconcerned at her formal linen suit she bought a cheap large sunhat, and, not yet feeling able to be bothered looking at any unfamiliar path, she walked slowly back to the harbour.

Oustaou de la Mer, Société Marseillaise de Crédit, Tabacs, Café de l'Escale. The church, and the houses, reminded her of a type of plastic interlocking blocks one sees in toyshops, called Lego.

Her sunglasses, the expensive type that do not darken, but turn glare into a clear grisaille pattern drawn with a fine pen on pale-grey paper, showed her a sailor walking down to the harbour, in boots and a faded cotton fatigue uniform. His childish mouth was adorned by a gay moustache that made him look even more downy and vulnerable. The uniform had shrunk – or he had grown – and his hands and boots looked enormous.

Showed her Michel, captain of *Bambi*, grey-haired and immaculate in his blue shirt and trousers and loose blue jacket. Very handsome, with a dapper dandified look. Startlingly unlike her notion of a sailor.

Showed her old Marius, quarrelling with somebody as usual, in a check tweed cap, a hairy sweater, several scarves, and woolly bedroom slippers. Perfectly calm and comfortable in the blazing sunlight.

Showed her Léon – his cap was beige, he had a woolly vest that buttoned up to the throat under his shirt, and a canary yellow sweater. His canvas jacket was much faded. For a change, he was wearing army boots.

All these sights gave her keen enjoyment. She would recover her pleasure in life, here. She stood still and looked out over the harbour.

Christophe and Raymond had finished painting *Olivia*, and were easing her down the rollers into the water, the crane taking the strain. Another extraordinary sight, she thought. What contrast could be greater than that between those two? Christophe was plainly a comic-opera sailor – practically Captain Haddock – and the other ... English? Swedish? That stork-like northern look, with bleached hair and bleached khaki trousers, rather shrunk. Both comic; the Frenchman with a theatrical buoyancy, the other with that characteristic worried stiffness. They were too busy to pay any attention to her; if they had, she would not have been embarrassed. She came from a world where people were accustomed to looking everybody over appraisingly, as one looks at a horse.

Raymond jumped lightly from the quayside to the deck. He felt better, this morning. Pride and warmth flowed again through him at standing again upon his own deck, feeling *Olivia* again alive and supple under his bare feet.

'I'll take her out to the mooring. Back in ten minutes. Apéritif at the Arche? Good – this time I pay.'

His eyes were caught by the woman's figure, standing indolent there on the shore. Admirable legs; pity one can't see under the hat, and more of what's behind those huge silly glasses. With a sudden gaiety – born of being again captain of his ship and himself, perhaps – he made her an impudent salute with his hand, no longer stiff.

Not knowing or caring why, enjoying herself, Natalie returned the wave, with equal impudence, which tickled Raymond – and Christophe, who had turned so as not to miss whatever it was. Eh – our serious captain. Natalie was strolling along the narrow strip of beach; Christophe observed the elegant mannered walk with interest. Who the hell could that be?

'Staying here?'

'Suddenly decided, it seems – she phoned Paris.'

'So Servaz is the real name, then?'

'I knew straight away. A year or so ago she was on the cover of *Match*.'

'I've seen her on the screen too.'

'Not a star, though.'

'Well no, but a good actress. More than these stars are.'

'Not a star, but a sort of – what d'you call it? No ice in yours, right? And, Monsieur Léon? Two pastis and a tomate?'

'A second lead.'

'That's the word I wanted. Not a tomate? – oh, a Mauresque.'

'A character actress. Like Signoret.'

'Have you seen her then, Charley?'

'Oh yes. I like. Couldn't see her hair though.'

'Black. Short.'

'Perfect.'

'They wear wigs.'

'Qué, wigs.'

'Well I've seen her in pictures with long hair. Ah good morning, Captain.'

'Morning, everybody,' said Raymond happily. 'Bet I know who you're talking about.'

'But we hear from Christophe that you are already old friends . . . Psst, here she comes.'

'Mandarin with a bit of lemon, Madame, please.'

Natalie accepted cautious stares with unconcern. Anyway it wasn't jealousy, here. She felt that here she would be accepted – if she played fair. They wouldn't be impressed by airs and graces. She took off her hat and glasses; everybody's eyes were riveted on her hair. She smiled across the bar at Madame, who was holding a bottle in her commanding way, as though it were a marshal's baton.

'Good morning, everybody. Thank you, Madame, a little Carpano. I had a fine walk, and observed the life of the harbour.'

'Aha,' pouring Raymond's drink, 'Monsieur Capitaine putting his boat back in the water, with Admiral Christophe to show him how.'

Christophe was just opening his mouth to say something witty when Raymond spoke.

'We have met – but only across fifty metres of water.'

Everyone was slightly astonished; Natalie found it comic. 'And now we have reduced the distance.'

'To that across a table?'

'If you wish.' She sat down; he picked up the drinks and brought them over.

'To Noah's Ark.'

'Oh – to other boats as well.' Madame had given him picon instead of mandarin, preoccupied. He was amused. Now they don't have to spend their whole lives thinking I'm no better than a beachcomber, do they?

He had acted out of vanity more than anything else. It was pleasant to astonish the Porquerollois, for once. He could see that she was sharp enough. She had been amused by his manoeuvre.

'That was a little naughty of you,' she said, in English. He was delighted; he was proud of his English, and it made a little private conspiracy out of his cheeky remark.

'But why should they have all the fun? I thought I would steal something from them for once. I think they know who you are, but I'm afraid I don't. Some sort of celebrity – you'll have to tell me, or they will triumph over my ignorance. I was shamed the other day – a very ordinary-looking boy who came in on a yacht, and I didn't know it was a prince. Not well up on the illustrated papers, you see. Perhaps you're a princess.'

She laughed, pleased with the little compliment as well as the joke. Really, he had done that quite well. Not so provincial, this boy.

'Long time since I've been in *Match*. Still, it's pleasant to be recognized. I'm a cinema actress, regarded as competent, in moderate demand.'

'So I am shamed, after all.'

'Not a bit. Being waved at is nice, and gratifying, after people who pretend to think, and then say "Surely your face is familiar".'

'So it's gratifying both being recognized and not being recognized?'

'Certainly.'

'Aha. I'm ahead of them all there at last.' This remark pleased her.

'Now you must tell me something. Really, this is the first time I've ever been on this coast – I don't count Cannes or Antibes. I'm wondering how it is possible that I've never noticed things. Why is it that the true native costume is a thick sweater and woolly bedroom slippers?'

It was his turn to be amused.

'It gets cold here in the evenings, and the early mornings – especially on the water. But the slippers – they baffle me too. Perhaps the fish don't hear them coming?'

'Aha. I see I shall have to study everything, here. I shall enjoy that.'

'Would you like another drink?'

'No indeed, thank you. I must go and wash. But I owe you a compliment. I'm alone here; you must tell me more things about this island. Why don't you come to dinner with me – say tomorrow night?'

It was a surprise to Raymond, an unexpected tribute. He was startled, but very pleased.

'I'd like that very much.'

'Let's take it as settled.' She held out her hand. 'Till then – at the hour of the apéritif, Monsieur ...'

'Kapitan. Raymond Kapitan.' She was gone. He paid for the drinks in high good humour. Hell, it's been a long long time since anybody invited me to dinner.

Natalie was laughing at herself slightly, drying her hands on a hotel towel. Well ... I take a room here, without having as much as pyjamas with me – she had left her car in Toulon – and the first thing I do is invite a total stranger to dinner. Typical Natalie. And what does it matter, after all? One comes to islands to do this kind of thing – what else is the point of them?

Raymond was grilling fish back at home. He was very hungry – lucky to have a good fish, a daurade of over a kilo, taken this morning. Good thing, he thought, that I am extremely fond of fish, because I get damn little else. He finished it the local way, dumping a bunch of dried herbs on top of the fish and setting it on fire, so that the fragrant ash mixed with the juice. He would invite that woman back here to the boat, he thought; she sounds extremely promising.

Tomorrow, mm; the Corse might be here tomorrow. Busy day for you, my lad, he thought. It was very calm fine weather; he would take *Olivia* out for a sail, and tonight he would set a net over on the south side of the island, in his favourite spot, the bay called in Provençal 'The House of God', because it was the only place on the whole south side of the island that gave any shelter when a mistral blew.

Good place to sleep, too. He got fed up with harbours sometimes, and instead of always looking over the Petite Passe, with the eye hemmed in on both sides, and the vulgar lights of Hyères after dark, there was only the limitless Mediterranean, and the revolving double beam of the powerful Porquerolles lighthouse launching a glitter every five seconds upon the oily water.

Chapter Five

There was nothing in the net worth speaking of, next morning, till at the very end he got a fair-sized langouste, which he was very pleased to see – it was worth a lot of money and he would certainly be able to sell it. It was a bore being poor. The Corse might help. And this woman ... she certainly had money; she was not only covered with the exterior marks of wealth but she had the assurance that only comes from the certainty that there is nothing you need deny yourself if you really want it badly. A cinema actress, after all. Could he possibly seduce her?

A greyish haze, like smoke, hung over the mainland, giving the coast an Irish look. Ireland – he had sailed *Olivia* up the west coast of Ireland, in the early days of the great plan. It was cheap there; he had been tempted by the superb anchorage, by the huge empty fjords and the seas swarming with fish and lobster. But he had been disheartened; the endless cold and damp – and the people had seemed to him a spiritless remnant in an empty land, with an endless flow of talk, but unable even to catch, let alone cook, the marvellous fish on their doorstep.

Perhaps it was only sun they needed – he knew that by mid-morning the sun would have eaten up the haze, however chill and grey it might look now.

He was happy at the idea of seeing the Corse, who was not just a fair-weather friend, and happy at the prospect of Natalie, but there was a stealthy rottenness in his heart, the same that was there, still, under *Olivia's* deck. What good was his life here, with no money? What good was the plan? Even if poor, he had always pinned his faith in the plan, but now – to mend the rotted hull, money was needed. A lot of money.

For years now, his days had been full with the plans for the trip round the Horn to Valparaiso – right across the South

Atlantic, right up the west coast of South America. Bit by bit, everything had been got ready – and now it was hopeless. What could he do? If only he had money.

Raymond lived upon an income that came to him from the uncle who had the cigar-shop, whom he had hardly known, who had no children of his own – the very uncle he had been afraid to borrow ten bob from, that day with Pauline. It was hateful – because of this uncle, he had never been able to forget Pauline, to cut himself free.

Raymond could remember him well enough, very broad and solid, with a bonhomous baby face, and tiny sharp eyes of a very pale grey, always with an amber cigar-holder in his mouth. There had been no sweets for children in the shop, but whenever he had been there he had been given one of the innumerable varieties of salt liquorice – little pointed diamonds, flat discs, the name stamped in a circle, little black cats. His favourite had been the bears, a tobacco-brown colour, harder and shinier than the others.

Father had not left a penny; the savings had melted in inflation and the pension died with him. But the uncle, with the shelves and shelves of cigars, with the lottery tickets, the racks of pipes, the tobacco pouches that smelt so lovely – the uncle his father had looked down on as a petty shopkeeper – had always lived alone, frugally, and had made a surprising quantity of money. And left it to his three nephews, in equal thirds. It was in investments, solid reliable ones with low dividends. The sort that never vary more than a fraction on the Bourse, never give bonus issues, never get taken over, never take risks, but are always there, as permanent and trustworthy as anything can be, in this world.

Raymond's third was pawed over by lawyers and tax-inspectors, mulcted as it seemed by innumerable money-lenders before it reached a bank where he had never even set foot – but it reached him at last as a meagre quarterly cheque. It was enough to keep him alive; he did not need to work for a living. It was enough for ten cigarettes and one apéritif a day. It could, occasionally, be made enough for a tin of paint, a coil of rope, or a bolt of canvas, paid for painfully, with quibbling and the promise of fish, in three or four instalments.

It was not enough for stores, and this was the reason – the open, obvious reason – why he had never left for Valparaiso.

For to face a couple of hundred days at sea, there was food needed. Dried fruit and vegetables, smoked fat bacon, salt cod – he knew that one cannot reckon on the fishing line – a few tins, a very few, carefully greased and wrapped, for emergencies, and the final provision of fresh lemons, for his jumping-off point in the Azores.

Why didn't he work? Why had he not saved money, when he had worked? It had, as always, gone on high life in restaurants, casinos, smart bars, where one met women like Natalie. Or Pauline.

His mind was running down a too well-known and unpleasant groove; he could not stop it.

His father, after the interview with Mr de Beaugency, had been no help. Raymond had expected as much; the trouble with this type of man, with respectable, legal jobs, is that they are in a constant panic lest the behaviour of their children compromise them. When one lives in a provincial town – even with a population of a million – one never quite gets away from the provincial disease; everybody knowing everybody else. The good man had been paralysed by the appearance of Mr de B.

'Really, you must bank the money. We would add whatever we were able to spare – it would pay for your board as well as studies. There's a very famous university there in Lisbon . . .' Raymond had flown into a rage. To twist his arm with a few miserable pennies – that thousand pounds was his, to do with as he pleased. Mr de B. had said so.

He was excited at the idea of Lisbon; it was a gay and beautiful town. And a capital; no more provincial manners. He was to stay there, off and on, four and a half years.

Mr de B.'s card worked extremely well. Telephone calls from a big airy office, with wonderful antique English furniture, got him living and working permits from the police, a comfortable and cheap lodging, a good job with a travel agency.

It worked a second time – somewhat. A job in a bookshop, after a long uncomfortable silence had passed across a fine Chippendale bureau in the private office.

The third time he was not even allowed in. Finally he got a job as a hotel porter, off his own bat. He found that giving the name as a reference did not work either.

But he did not lack all sense. He lived on what he earned, and his thousand pounds did not melt in fripperies. Sometimes he ate into it, a little, but then he saved till he had got it back. It was sacred, somehow. He earned well, by local standards, life was cheap, and he always contrived to manage. A tall, northern-looking young man, presentable and intelligent, speaking French and English and German, learning Spanish as well as Portuguese, could always keep above water, then. He travelled about, had a good life, and it was a fine thing to have a thousand pounds to spend when, one day, he found *Olivia*.

He had formed the idea of buying a boat after a series of misfortunes with lodgings. It was only the idea of a houseboat, a living boat, at first. Landladies ate him up, destroyed him. They made a fuss about girls and keys and food; they robbed him of privacy, of independence, as well as of money. Some kind of boat was the answer, he had thought. With a boat, one paid no rent, and harbour dues were very small. The weather was no problem, and maintenance very little.

Not exactly a fishing boat – but along those lines, with some sort of cabin. He fell into the habit of stopping to look at boats, and mixing with the harbour crowd that lived by them. Yachts often came from England and Belgium – even from as far as Sweden; it roused his imagination that one could, apparently without great difficulty, bring a small boat round Ushant and down the French coast, and even enjoy it.

But he found nothing that corresponded with the ideal. Boats of the type he envisaged had cabins like match-boxes, where one perched in damp and cramp; that wasn't the idea at all. He started thinking of something bigger.

An acquaintance, an amateur yachtsman of the dinghy-sailing, hang-out-to-windward type, gave him a roneoed sheaf of papers one day: 'Found that in the British Consulate; thought it might be something for you, perhaps.' Admiralty Small Craft Disposals, read the heading.

All sorts of exciting-sounding things, all for sale apparently, all at cheap prices. Most were in England of course, but quite a few nearer home. Tugs, harbour tenders – one at Gibraltar – a ninety-foot German E-boat, with her original Maybach diesels, at La Rochelle. Too big alas, and too dear. But there were two sixty-foot launches, ex-Air-Sea-Rescue-tenders, with no motors, but very cheap – and lying at Vigo. It was not far; he decided to go to Vigo at the weekend.

It took a good deal of trouble; nobody seemed to know who was looking after them. But at last he found a boatyard – or scrapyard rather. It was siesta-time; the place was deserted, but he unearthed a greasy-overalls character who spoke Portuguese with a Portsmouth accent and introduced himself as 'the engineer'.

'These launches . . .'

'Can't go to sea. No engine. Oh, to live on. I can tell you about that – I'm living on one myself. Bloody awful. Sweats like hell – steel hull, y'see – and y'fry in summer. Want to buy a boat, do you? Sell y'mine, if y'like.'

He had come all that way; might as well look.

'There's the launches, right? Moored to the buoys there in the fairway. Now see the black boat alongside? She's mine.'

It seemed very tiny.

'Ah, but wait'll y'see how she's fixed inside. Good boat. M'wife don't want to sell'r, but I need the money. Row you out, to see?'

The boat was *Olivia*. Ten minutes after stepping on the shabby, solid deck, Raymond had found the love-affair of his life. And an hour later he had made up his mind. He saw her papers and a recent survey. She was Lloyd's-registered, and the price was seven hundred pounds. He told the man he would let him know.

Even if she was dear at the price, he would buy her. But he learned she was relatively cheap. A working boat, with all her rigging and gear. The man took nothing out of her – Raymond got a dinghy, anchors, a tremendous litter of wire, cable, and half-full pots of paint. The man took a barometer – Raymond brought everything he had. He made a clean sweep; he left his job, he left everything. From that moment, *Olivia* was his home and his life.

Learning was painful at first. He had unhappy awakenings in a smelly rubbish-heap before he learned to clean up as he went. And he took ludicrous risks, through inexperience. Landfalls at night in unknown harbours, and getting too close to rocky lee-shores. He had to learn right from the beginnings of elementary seamanship: that whatever the risks and terrors of the open sea, they are always less than those of shoal water and a tide rip off a headland. He was fantastically lucky – several times.

But when he learned to get out of sight of land and take star-sights, it was a fine thing to put one's trust in a good boat. To be at sea, real sea with water a mile deep under the keel, and lay head to wind in a blow – that obliterated Pauline. He had never heard of her again.

He worked, always to the same pattern. It was exciting to get jobs, to learn them once got, but after three months, the details mastered, he lost interest. Mostly he left, then. Sometimes he got fired for insolence – and once at least for fiddling the expenses. He learned something about journalism, and did well out of the first boom year of Spanish tourism. He sank to selling Moroccan leatherwork in the Balearics, and rose again to conducted tours of the Bordeaux wine country – with tasting.

Sometimes he had crises of despair. The worst was when he tried to join the Foreign Legion, and got turned down for having flat feet.

Even in Tangier he never did anything really downright dishonest, though he would if anyone had given him the chance to smuggle Jews, or guns, or gold. He was involved in some squalid little schemes, and had his boat searched four times by French, English, and Spanish authorities. He got to know the Atlantic coasts well, and the western half of the Mediterranean.

He generally earned good wages when he worked. With his polite manners and respectable looks, a knowledge of languages and neat paperwork, he could get jobs in hotels when all failed. He learned about policemen and consular officials, customs men and all likely employers. He had many little adventures with women tourists.

Once or twice he had real windfalls, and would go to Paris until he had no penny left and had to hitch-hike back to wherever *Olivia* was moored, awaiting his return.

He got the letter quite by accident – from a vice-consul in Oporto. It invited him to convey his whereabouts to a firm of notaries back in the almost forgotten town of his youth; he did, and got a legacy out of it. A remarkable piece of luck, that – it might have been years before he was back in Oporto.

Not Pa – trust Pa to leave nothing. Good old Uncle Gustav in the cigar-shop.

Had it just been the nephews because the old boy had no children of his own? Or had he had some lingering sympathy for this beachcomber, who possessed none of the shopkeeper's virtues? It would have been easy to show disapproval by forgetting, conveniently.

Had Uncle Gustav sometimes smelt the trade wind, in a cedarwood box of Cuban cigars?

When Raymond learned, through chilly legal letters, that he had an income, from another man's forty years of honest trade, he had already formed the Plan. But why Valparaiso? True, he had learned that only a Mediterranean climate is livable. It is the only place in all South America that has one. But that was a minor point.

Perhaps because of his reading. One book – he had forgotten author, title, even subject – had left a phrase tattooed upon his inner skin: 'The Innsbruck-like funiculars, and butterfly-haunted streets of Santiago.'

It continued to haunt him, even after his farthest penetration into the Mediterranean, which landed him off the most southerly point of France, the little group of islands known prosaically as the Iles d'Hyères.

There were months on end when he did not think at all of Valparaiso. But he went on fitting *Olivia* for an ocean passage, studying geography and meteorology in the libraries of Hyères and even Toulon. Working out stores and sail-plans. Thinking of emergencies and warm clothes that he had not needed in ten years.

What else had he to do?

There was *Sparrowhawk* over there on the horizon, five minutes out from Giens. She would be here in ten; he wrapped his langouste up carefully and slid into the dinghy. Three or four days ago, he had had a scrawled card, from the Corsican. His friend, as far as he had one. Well, Christophe was a friend too, perhaps. When one thought of it, Christophe was as close as the Corse was. Nobody ever got any closer.

'Holà, Jo.'

'Holà, Ramon.'

'Come – we will have a glass. But first, I have a tiny scrap of business to attend to.' And indeed, it was very handy to have caught that langouste. It would pay for drinks, and an extra packet of cigarettes, not only now but tonight, with Natalie. It made him free, and not just a beggar. With the Corse, it was important not to be a penniless poor fellow.

As always, Jo presented his highly personal style. Looking at him, one always wondered whether two totally different plants had not been here blended by some Mendelian freak. The foliage was strange, the flowers vivid, the fruit both sweet and sharp, but with a peculiar after-taste. Perhaps poisonous, who knew? There were so many strange fruits, exotic flowers, odd spiky leaves among the agaves and lentisks of the Côte d'Azur.

What was the real character of the Corse – what were his real capabilities? A loyal friend, and a good man on your side in a fight. More. How was it that this gangster-boy, this delinquent juvenile, had become a friend of his? He would have found it difficult to answer the plain question. In Jo's company, he would have been uneasy at being seen by Natalie. He would not even have been quite happy at Christophe's joining them. This Corsican boy was something he kept a little secret, as though he felt just a little guilty.

He was not much more than a boy. Perhaps twenty-four, five. Small and thin. Hard as a board though, and quick as a trout. Bright electric-blue eyes under matted black brows that met together. The top half of the face might have been just a fisher-boy's; the mouth and chin were sensitive, certainly. There was intelligence in the face, but the dominant impression always was that the blend was a little imperfect, had not quite come off.

The clothes, too, betrayed the blend. The Corse always wore the tight blue sailcloth trousers, stained and faded, of every harbour hanger-on, but his shirts and sweaters were always amusing, gay fantasies from expensive shops. His hair was long and careless, but he was always fastidiously shaved and spotless clean, smelling lavishly of good eau-de-Cologne. All Corsicans, from Napoleon down, have a resemblance, and all are devoted to eau-de-Cologne.

Raymond felt as he always did in the Corse's company. Faded and bleached, ten years older and slower, needing energy, needing force, awkward, and weary. This boy Jo was frightened of nothing, would stop at nothing, would surmount everything, to succeed, to do whatever it was he had set his hand to.

When he got back, the Corse was sitting on the terrace with a whole row of drinks in front of him, royal, expansive.

'You're in the money.'

'Certainly I am in the money. We will have drinks, we will eat dinner. But after eating, we go to the boat. I have projects, for which I need your advice. But I wish no waving ears. We can talk here, and have a good dinner, first. I have plenty money, that is not important.'

'It is to me; I'm low at present.'

'I cannot understand you – why do you choose to live like this? On this potty island where nothing happens. No life, no company. At Saint-Trop, or Cannes, you could quickly make fortune.'

'No. I need solitude. I prefer it here. I can think, I can fish, I have quiet.'

'Me,' flatly, 'I cannot sleep without a woman in my bed. But you are a strange one. Not like the others.'

'Where are you living then? Still in Saint-Trop? By old Mother Tripeguts?'

'I spit on Mother Tripeguts. I have a cabin of my own, on a yacht, moored as always in Cannes harbour. The life of a gentleman. You understand – I have as well a room on the port, for women. On the yacht, not possible . . .' He flicked his fingers in a tiny gesture of wariness, the little bird that flies away.

The life of a gentleman. Raymond had to laugh at that. Jo, who had never eaten anything but polenta and ratatouille in his life, till Raymond had shown him how to hold a knife and fork, and not to put his elbows on the table and talk with his mouth full. And now. On a yacht in Cannes harbour? What sort of yacht could that be?

'I have photographs, I have all sorts of things.' The Corse gestured vaguely at the beach-bag he always carried. 'I show you, later. We eat, we go out to the boat, we drink coffee there. Right?'

'Put the kettle on, then. Not sea-water, like last time you were here.'

'That was last time,' negligently. 'I know now the life of the yacht.'

'How did you get over here, from Cannes?'

'Aha. My big, my great surprise. I came specially to announce it. I have now an auto. Not a filthy tin can, second-hand, but a real English sport auto. Triumph cabriolet, twelve hundred, very chic, red and grey. On the corniche – a tomahawk. One might almost believe a Porsche, a Giulietta . . .'

'And where did this come from?'

'My American. My yacht owner. My lover, ha. A present. Disinterested present.' The Corse smiled; youthful, innocent, wicked.

Raymond saw light.

'Ah – a pédé.'

'Naturally. Americans have no capacity for women, their women in addition terrorize them – all are pédé, all. This one is nice – you know, civilized.'

It was one of Raymond's words – it sounded comic in the boy's mouth.

'Loves the good life, loves France of course, has immense

quantities – immense, I tell you – of money. I show you the photos.' Out of the beach-bag came a pile of glossy prints. The first were of a sleek white motor-yacht, ninety-footer. No sort of a sea-boat, but very pretty.

Raymond snorted. 'Poor man's *Christina*.'

'Believe – inside, she is superb. But look farther.'

On the deck, groups, couples, a party. In all the groups, in shorts – meagre, with a wrinkled body like dried mud – in white suits, in evening clothes, in Hawaiian costumes, figured an elegant grey man with a little pointed beard, a cigar, large expensive rings. In one of the photos he was accompanied by two women with the same sort of figure – slim, dried-out, over-tanned. They were fortyish; one smoked a cigar too, and smiled a bony smile. They wore large hats, much elaborate jewellery, bikini bottoms, were bare-breasted.

In one of the party photos Raymond recognized Jo, dressed up to kill, holding a big glass of Scotch and ice-cubes, dancing with the host.

'Ha.'

'Am I not superb?' said the Corse, with magnificence.

'Not a girl in sight.'

'No. But we have charming guests. Last night to dinner, a lesbian very famous; première danseuse, it appears, of London Opera.'

'What's his name?'

'Vincento. He is a fine fool. I feed him with hopes. The hopes he lives in, I defer, adroitly, you may be sure. He loves me tenderly. And meanwhile I have a new girl. A beautiful English girl. A lily of the valley.'

You've never even seen a lily of the valley, thought Raymond, crossly, except maybe on a flower-stall the last day of April. But he had to laugh tremendously at the idea. The Corse, wooed and spoiled by an elderly wealthy American pederast, at table drinking expensive wine, and eating little birds off skewers, on white linen, in an air-conditioned saloon, in a motor-yacht in Cannes harbour.

Amazing. But amusing. He enjoyed the idea of the Corsican – thanks to patient teaching – learning to live under protective colouring in the gardens of the rich. A jungle animal, prowling on the soft earth of flowerbeds, climbing quiet and supple up the creepers outside bedroom windows.

Nothing he asked better. Let the Corse sink his teeth in their throats, the lot of them, and fulfil simultaneously his simple ambition of making 'an immense fortune'.

'So. And now you have a lily of the valley, a new auto, and a cabin on the yacht. Was I right or not in telling you to stay away from all that cheap crowd?'

It really was intensely funny ... this boy, who had never known anything finer, before meeting Raymond, than sitting at a plastic-topped table next to the pinball machine, drinking Campari-soda and eating stewed tripe. What would be next?

'I have nothing more to do with them.'

'And the crowd in Saint-Trop? The loves? The Karina Dominique?'

'Sighs. Weeps. I sweep past. No no, I do not sweep past – you know I am faithful to my friends, even to la Dominique, la Karina. But that crowd of riffraff, of good-for-nothings, I have no further use for. I bought them all a drink, and the eyes of those parasites followed me, eating me up, pouring upon me the acid of their envy. I remain impervious. Still, I am grateful to the lovely Dominique. I will give her to you if you like. She is domestic, she will do the washing.'

How could the stupid boy know that Raymond had no use for any woman on the boat? Even Dominique, a magnificent girl with splendid skin and curves, lovely chestnut hair and really fine blue eyes. A drunken English boy, just learning his first mouthful of Italian, had named her 'la bella iocchi' – the name had stuck, ever since, along the coast.

'Give me another cup of coffee,' said Raymond lazily. 'What is the new one called?'

'Patricia. You will see – it is superb. Small, fragile ...' The Corse was tongue-tied by lyricism, Astonishing, thought Raymond. The boy had a vocabulary of about five hundred words when I knew him first, in a sort of god-forsaken Genoese dialect that wasn't Italian, or French, or even Provencal; one could scarcely understand the uncouth young animal. Yet even then bursting with confidence, and a fierce wish to know. The first time he was aboard the boat, he had looked at the books, and then at me, as though I were a witch-doctor.

The Corse was scrabbling in the beach-bag, and came up with a sweater-shirt of fine wool, the kind with buttons and a collar, a soft autumn brown-gold colour.

'For you. Vin bought it for me, but it does not suit my colouring; on you it will look good.' Becoming an artist, too.

'Now look, Ramon, I have come to talk business; we must plan further. Very interesting people come to the yacht. I see much, I hear much. I have projects. If I succeed – you have taught me very much; as a Corse, I do not forget. But you are obstinate – you insist on staying here; you are poor and will not grow rich. Why not come with me? We can plan – for that I need your head, your experience.'

'Plan what? More of your notions that we'll all go to jail for?'

'No no. But there is no gaining a fortune without certain small risks. For instance, many of these imbeciles drug themselves. I know who supplies the première danseuse: it is a Catalan whom I knew in Monte Carlo; you recall the affair of the camera. What is to prevent our supplying these people? We have the boat – it is a question of a trip to Tunis every three months, no more. We would need capital, but I have thought . . .'

'Do what you please,' interrupted Raymond in a cold, detached voice.

'But, Ramon. They would never think of looking at your boat. It is a perfect cover.'

'I won't use the boat for contraband. I have my own life; I'm not interested.'

The Corsican was abashed.

'Ah. For you . . . But I tell you, I must advance, I must progress.'

'Possibly. I use my head. I have my boat, I am my own master, I do as I please. Shall I risk that in some three-ha'penny contraband? Have you never seen the coastguard boats? The machine-gun they carry on the deck? Have you seen their spotter helicopter? They confiscate the goddam boat. Who'll give me a new one? You?'

'But, Ramon, how should they know?'

'They get tipped off. Somebody sees or hears, always. Who tells a girl. Who tells the whole port. It gets to Massabielle. Who doesn't need to do a damn thing, but who gives a little phone call to his very good friend the Commissaire in Toulon.'

The Corsican got angry.

'Good. I know you are right and you are smart. But I am not going to stay like those miserables, I am going to make a fortune, I am going to make myself respected, I am not going to end my life with flat feet and no penny as a barman, peuchère.'

'Té, té, I've told you to leave the little silly tricks, that the police rumble without even turning over in bed, to fools, right? And you agree. Now I tell you to leave big stuff to the big boys, like Massabielle – they have the organization, the capital. Their lawyers, their friends in the administration. Their respectable lives. Big house, big auto, very quiet careful life. Who could ever accuse Massabielle of handling narcotics – as everybody knows he does – when he never even sees it, or touches it? If anybody gets hit, it's your precious Catalan. You want to be a fool like that?'

'But how did Massabielle start?'

'With a good three-year stretch, and making friends with everybody he met there,' indifferently. 'More than that I don't know, and I don't care, what's more. It seems to me smarter to rob somebody – a legal way. Give them what they think they want – if they want to pay for it that's their lookout. If you're a chemist, sell them stuff to get brown. If you're a tailor, sell them shirts with pictures on. If you've nothing, think of something new. Shells, bits of vinewood – they're fool enough to buy anything.'

It was all a waste of breath, but Raymond did not care. He wasn't interested anyway.

'You aren't doing badly for a start. Selling illusions – nothing illegal about that.'

He was bore and needed amusement; he changed the subject.

'I'll bring the boat over one of these days. Cannes's too far –

perhaps Saint-Trop. We'll have a few drinks. Bring Dominique – she amuses me.'

'Sure. Give me a phone-call any time – the café on the port will take the message. If you get any ideas, you tell me then?'

'Yes,' said Raymond.

After Jo had gone, he set himself to wash up and polish the lino, to have everything again spotless and tidy. He wasn't competing with *Christina*. But if he had not *Olivia*, what was there left? He would be lower than the Corsican, who had money and a sport auto. He would lounge about the waterfront in a fancy sweater, like the riffraff in Saint-Tropez, who thought him pretty smart because he owned his own boat and did no work.

Chapter Six

Natalie's luggage had arrived on the morning boat, with the Corsican. She put on shorts and walked over to the cliffs on the south side of the island, where she saw a big lizard sunning himself on a rock. She amused herself by seeing how close she could get before he became aware suddenly of her stealthy feet, and vanished with a flick of his powerful tail.

She was happy to be alone here. Fred, her husband, might decide to come for a weekend when he learned she was here, but it was a place for being alone. A place for silence among the pines and myrtles, for feeling the warmth on her skin and under her feet, for letting a still, salt sea carry her without effort, let her feel for once that she need not swim so breathlessly to keep afloat. This island pleased and amused her. She had not regretted her invitation to Raymond; on islands there were always odd characters – perhaps romantic, comic characters – who lived on boats and were beachcombers. Anyway, she was an actress, she was interested in character. She was even a much better actress, she thought sometimes, than anybody gave her credit for. Lot of good it did her. Nobody wanted actresses now, for the cinema. They were old-fashioned. Films were made by neurotic boy geniuses now, who were not interested in acting. They were only concerned about how much their precious scenarios reflected their own paltry egos. Imbeciles.

Why hadn't she had the luck to get there earlier, before this potty new cinema began? In the days of Jouvet, or René Clair.

Maybe I wouldn't have needed, then, to launch myself into these extraordinary relationships with people, Natalie told herself. It's as if I were constantly engaged in filming little private scenarios on my own account. Very ridiculous.

Never mind. Whether my whims turn out well or ill, I am

not going to be fool enough to regret them. I am not going to regret anything, ever. My life is a well, out of which I draw a never exhausted stream of value. Everything I have ever done I have lived, faced, accepted. To the uttermost. I have often been very happy; I thank God for that. Very silly, no? I don't really believe in God, but I thank him for all that.

Will this island bring me adventures? I am sure it will; islands are the classical places for romantic adventures. This man ... how will this turn out? Not an anticlimax; I will make certain of that.

When I am old and finished I will have a whole life full of memories. I will recall bitter treasons, terrible pains, but I will laugh, I will be happy. It will not have been a poor life, or mean.

Even if I were to die here on this island, I will have lived. This man, this Capitaine, as the islanders call him with a sort of affectionate irony – will he love me? Will I love him? Why is there irony in their voices? Is it something more for me to learn, to live?

She had not brought a swimming suit with her, but she would like to swim. She wasn't going to strip like a silly girl, even if there was nobody here. Now why not? She was on an island; it was time to begin doing the things one only did on islands. She had no towel either; the sun would dry her.

She undressed and waded into the water. It was cold at first, with a bite, a grip, but she lay on the surface and let the sea – a clear pale emerald this morning – rock her. One must have confidence in the water, she thought, as in life, or the sun, or a dry shirt.

On her way back to the village, Natalie noticed that the water, or the sun, or both, had enormously increased her pleasure and her sharpness of observation. Everything was clear and precise, as things are on this coast at the end of a strong mistral. That eucalyptus tree, with the messy look that these trees always have, was astonishingly beautiful. She stopped to observe it: the splashes of green and silver-grey on the trunk, the pinkish-purple, banana-shaped leaves, the rubbish of bark in long strips lying everywhere around.

Even more so were the outskirts of the village, seen from the little hill of Sainte-Agathe. That is not a Provençal village, she told herself. It is a stage-set by Bakst. Yet it is completely lacking in artificiality. A white house had its wooden shutters painted horizon blue; another was bluish-white, the shutters marine blue. There was a rust red with peacock blue, a cream with orange, a dark cream with leaf green. The beauty, taste, and flair of all this was extremely astonishing. How is it possible? Natalie asked herself. Has someone made a film here? I am going to make one.

She had a shower, noticing that the maker's name was 'Queroy; Paris', and lay on her bed, wrapped in a towel, smoking a cigarette with enjoyment. This evening she was going to have dinner with – perhaps – a new lover. What would she wear? No make-up – she never did, except at work; it did nothing for her. A dress? No. A suit? – that nice shantung one. No; he would only think she had a girdle on under it. Trousers – grey ones; they always amused her. Nothing more entertaining than every inch of one being covered in very well cut, very tight trousers. Nor was she, like most women, afraid of sitting down in them.

She did not know it, but she had been sold, rather craftily, the langouste that Raymond had taken that morning, for their dinner.

Natalie was rather pleased that he had taken the trouble to dress up a little. She did not much care for men who are perpetually open and hairy just because they are in the south of France. She was, too, a woman from Paris. Beachcombers may be amusing, but not at dinner. Raymond had to pass a sort of test.

He passed it well. He never looked disreputable; he had always bought good clothes and looked after them, and however poor he might be he disgraced nobody. His ash-grey linen suit was years old but well cut, and he had put on a precious shore-laundered shirt. He smelt clean too, if not as luxurious as the Corse. Natalie approved of all this; she was also entertained by the glances of surprise he got from the islanders. Madame, a sturdy hippy woman with blonde hair and clever eyes, with a lot of chin, stomach, and character, gave him a look to count the matches in his box. She was measuring whisky into someone's glass, her mouth sticking out in a powerful concentration on business.

'What is it you drink?' asked Natalie contentedly. 'Two please, Madame.'

The two glasses tonked together comfortably. She had very quick, vivid black eyes. His, the colour of cigarette smoke, studied her appreciatively. The television set behind the bar was discussing Rugby football noisily; Madame reached up a hand and turned the sound down. Behind them, four Porquerollois in bedroom slippers were playing 'belotto'.

'What will I be able to do to return this?' he inquired. 'Do you like sailing? – oh, very quiet sailing, no need for energy. Our strong point is being slow but dignified.'

'As long as it's as nice as you make it sound. No hurry. This evening there are serious projects, such as langouste – I'm told it's a very good one that just came in this morning.'

'Mm'; he chalked up a mark to Madame, who was innocently polishing a glass. 'Lovely. One doesn't see many of them – we're in luck.'

'You know this island well?'

'I've been here – yes, very nearly a year.'

'Without ever going away?'

The black eyes were curious, but not just inquisitive, he thought. He liked direct women. That obliqueness that they practise – if they knew how boring it was.

'Without ever going away.'

'You are fond of this island?'

'The place is notorious for people who come for a week and stay six months.'

'Yes, I wouldn't be at all surprised to see it happen to me. You'll have to advise me about the symptoms. I climbed up this afternoon to the semaphore – wonderful. I don't only mean the view. One could see all the bones of the island from above, through all those boring pine-trees.' He looked at her with interest. 'Oh look, we're being called, the animal must be ready.'

'I wonder' – she was having a little rest in the middle of her langouste – 'whether you find me too personal – asking questions like that. It comes perhaps of living too much in the cinema world. Savages. No manners, and a trick of asking personal things, and making personal comments, as a sort of game: who blushes first.'

'Doesn't bother me.'

'Your life is no concern of mine – you might be very sensitive to questions about it.'

'Maybe I am,' said Raymond. Really, he thought, have I been isolated so long, with nothing to look at but little provincial girls, that I should forget how to talk to a woman from Paris? 'Let's say I won't answer any questions here – on the boat would be another matter.'

She mopped at tarragon-flavoured, lobstery butter with a piece of rather stale bread – it was closing day for the Porquerolles baker.

'If you won't regret asking me, I'll accept your offer then, to go sailing.'

'Being on the water makes answering questions easy.'

'As long as I don't have to watch you fishing – men who fish bore me very much.'

'My fishing's done strictly at night.'

'Good. Am I mistaken, or is this wine extremely strong?' It was a Coteaux des Baux called 'Mas de la Dame', and was extremely strong.

'I seem to be dropping suddenly with sleep.'

'Blame the langouste – he won't mind.'

'And the semaphore. What about tomorrow?'

'I'll wait for you in the harbour with the dinghy.'

'I won't keep you waiting,' she promised.

'Listen,' said Raymond, helping her in – the dinghy had been carefully baled out and then scrubbed – 'I've got something to eat, but not very grand; I'm generally rather poor.' She had a large beach-bag, full of he wondered what.

The eyes glinted with slightly malicious humour.

'My, what stiff northern manners. But I'm fairly rich, and knowing you were poor – not a secret specially, hm? – I thought I'd be more welcome if I brought things to eat – and drink. The rest of all this baggage you're eyeing so apprehensively is only clothes, in case I'm too hot, or too cold, or get sunburnt – or fall in.'

Raymond resisted these attacks.

'Somehow I can't see you falling in.'

There was a little wind this morning, enough to ruffle the water of the Passe. *Olivia*, heeled a little under all her very plain sail, made a long board out to sea after rounding the point, and headed over towards Levant.

'What's the name of that island?'

'Port-Cros. Nothing special to see there, unless you are very interested in bushes. The garrigue, very rocky and thorny.'

'With regret, no.'

'But I thought we'd go round the far side. This side's all cliffs, but there's a bay on the other side, and shelter enough to keep the boat still: we can eat without falling into the soup.'

She sat alongside him in the cockpit, in three-quarter sail-cloth trousers and a marine-blue sweater. She was deft in the boat, not in the way, giving no little shrieks, and not the least inclined to be sick.

'The only actresses I've ever known,' said Raymond meditatively, 'spent most of their lives, as far as I could see, standing in queues outside agents' offices.'

She smiled.

'I see I exaggerated my false modesty. I'm glad to say I belong to the type that doesn't have to queue. People do still sometimes give me phone calls. My trouble is I'm over thirty. The public has a mania for very young actresses. When I started in this business I was already too old. Otherwise maybe you would have heard of me.'

'But at least I don't belong to the public that only likes very young actresses. Are you a good actress?'

'Quite fair, but nobody wants actresses, good or bad, nowadays. An actor is, in modern films, a part of a more or less decorative but quite undramatic pattern. You may be in a scene – most carefully posed – with a flower or a gun or an old railway engine, and all three are more important than you are. It gives me, personally, the sick. Cinema has become hopelessly pretentious, and the producer comes to mean more than the actors. They don't talk about last films, they say, 'Oh yes, you were a railway engine in So-and-so's last but two, weren't you?'

'You are at home in a boat – you'd be a good sailor.'

'I daresay I'd be as frightened as anyone if there were waves. We're just gliding effortlessly, aren't we? But if we had to fight? I'd be petrified.'

'Anybody is petrified at first. Sometimes I dream of an enormous wave – they happen sometimes in the South Seas after earthquakes. On a calm sea, and from quite far off, I see it advancing towards me. I get up then for a drink of water.'

'But here, is there anything frightening?'

'Yes. There aren't huge waves, but there are very sudden dangerous storms. It's worse than being in the Atlantic.'

'Really? How?'

'Nobody quite understands when I say that, but there the waves are huge but long – even. A good boat goes up with them, no more effort than a seagull.'

She looked at him with amusement, and with a kind of respect.

'You've done that, then. You speak with knowledge, and the proper kind of pride.'

'Yes, I've done it: this boat is built for that. I'm proud of the boat – not of myself.'

Whatever she might have been going to say she changed her mind.

'Is this a mistral? It seems very inoffensive.'

'It's what the weather bureau describes as "Slight". Enough to keep the boat sailing, and keep one's sweater on. Once we're the other side of this island we'll find a sheltered bay.'

And indeed, *Olivia* came to a dignified stop a dozen metres off shore, surrounded by trees and bushes that came right to the water's edge. Even the dinghy only idled a pace or so on a slack painter; the whole of life appeared to have sunk, here, into a gentle doze. A single seagull planed leisurely overhead; there was no soul to be seen.

They ate in the cabin, and Natalie looked around her with surprise, fascinated as any person is by their first sight of a deep-water sailing boat from the inside. Everything is designed to stay in place and keep working, even if the boat should stand on end. She was charmed by the 'gimbals' – the brass ball-and-socket that forms a universal joint and keeps a lamp upright no matter what. It fascinated her that a décor could exist so decorative and yet so utterly stripped of the precious, the pretentious, and the false. A good sailing boat is as near absolute truth and beauty as the human being can get. One sees this – even now – if one looks at *Cutty Sark* in her dry-dock at Greenwich. The saloon is hardly bigger than Raymond's cabin.

It seemed strange to Natalie that she understood something of this. She had the habit of detachment of the true Parisian woman. Behind the universal mockery, they have springs of generosity that can be touched, but only by something completely genuine. They can recognize moments like this, and salute them. Natalie thought she was taking off her hat to Raymond when in reality she was admiring *Olivia*.

'It is a very serious boat.'

'Shouldn't it be?' Raymond was eating ham – the 'piquenique' she had brought – with appetite. 'It's a serious affair, a boat. There is a lot of work.'

'Just that it seems, somehow, not what one would expect, in these surroundings, I mean. A boat like this, for fishing – a bit like a rifle to catch grasshoppers.'

There was nothing hostile in her meaning, but the words stuck in Raymond like a flight of arrows, skewering him.

'Who said I wanted to catch grasshoppers?'

'What else is it that one does, here?'

He did not answer, but sank into a broody silence. Natalie wondered what she had said wrong. She lit a cigarette, and studied the books on the shelf.

He lit a cigarette himself and seemed to make a kind of effort.

'With a boat like this, one can make a very long voyage. A small boat – it's a question of the mechanics of waves – is even more easy than a big one. Across the Atlantic, say. Farther, even. You won't ever have heard of him, but thirty years ago a Frenchman called Gerbault went round the world on a boat no bigger than this – nowhere near as good a boat, either. He wrote books about it, which I possess – you're staring at them.'

Natalie stared at him, looking startled.

'Alone?'

'Certainly, alone. Isn't that the point? Being alone is what one needs. One must make a lot of careful preparations, and one needs a year's training. Gerbault did his training here, in the Mediterranean.'

French actors rather despise the 'actors' studio's' somewhat laborious methods. They do not need three days' walking along the beach to get into a storm mood. Natalie instantly saw the figure opposite her with a beard, eyes red with salt and sleeplessness – was she overacting? – tied with a rope in the little cockpit where she had elegantly crossed her knees. No, that was a mistake. She concentrated on the things around her, the everyday, familiar things she knew; plates, glasses, knives. Everything going up – swoosh – would it be like a fast lift? – going down – that sensation of one's stomach left sticking to the ceiling. How much, up and down? Thirty feet? She had no idea. She tried to see the Atlantic, and got stuck on bright-coloured parasols, on the beach at Sables-d'Olonne.

She decided that her wild-man-of-the-woods picture was that of a film unit's make-up man. She could imagine nothing but melodrama: a man crawling across the floor with his head cut open, blood trickling through matted hair. Sea-water sweeping the deck, crashing down the open hatch above her head. Absurd, lurid – a biblical epic no doubt, in cinemascope, starring last year's Mister World, with gigantic muscles and no penis. Huge glaring sunsets, livid pale dawns, a tiny boat endlessly bobbing on a vast oily mass of endlessly heaving water. She could not picture any reality. But – take away all that big production – perhaps she could picture an ideal. Ideals of this kind were a bit Victor Hugo, weren't they?

'Is that what you are going to do?' pleased to hear her voice had a perfectly normal tone.

'Yes ... You know the English money? Those huge heavy copper coins?'

'Yes. Pennies.'

'You've noticed that one gets them sometimes very old. Blackened, worn completely smooth – as though they'd been under water, but dirty. Effaced, and the dirt is sort of slick. The head is no more than a shadow – they're horrible. I feel like that, sometimes. But in South America – it is sharp. Not trodden on till there is nothing left but a kind of ghost.'

Not quite so Victor Hugo.

Raymond's words, once he had been stung into speaking about this, were coming easier.

'Why not just take a plane, you'll probably say.'

'But I think I understand. We are too European. But if one had seen nobody, and nothing but sea, for weeks I suppose, months perhaps, it would be right.'

'I think a lot about the first Spanish sailors. They went round the Horn to reach the Pacific, without even knowing what was on the other side. Think – they got right up beyond the Gulf of California, which is a horrible piece of water. The Sea of Cortez.'

'They trusted in God, and saints, and Jesuits.'

'Well,' flatly, 'I can see their point myself. Down there in the south, by the Horn, it is cold. There is ice, and always fog, and things in the fog. Voices. Haunts.'

She recovered a proper Parisian scepticism.

'Qué, voices. Seabirds, perhaps.'

He startled her by getting angry.

'Don't be a damned fool. When you are warm, and well fed, and in a comfortable bed, of course there are no haunts. But when you're alone, and it's blown a gale for ten days without stopping, and you don't know where you are because the sky isn't open enough to take a sight – then there are. You've had three half-hours of sleep in forty-eight, and your clothes are wet, and you have cold corned beef out of a tin for your main meal, and then you run into fog ... I tell you there are things there that will break your bones and suck the juice out.' He cut himself off, abruptly.

'Go on,' she said.

'You have weeks, you see, in the trade wind, first. It's warm and comfortable and quiet. Being alone is a pleasure. You fish, and darn your socks, and sing songs. It's like a boy's book – "it is, it is a glorious thing to be a pirate king".

'Then, bit by bit, you lose the wind. It gets quiet and still, and you start noticing frost on the deck in the mornings. Then one day there is snow – very fine hard powdery snow. Then you start wishing you'd never been born. You wish you had a few saints with you, then.'

Natalie realized that her mouth was slightly open.

'So you are ready to go,' she said, 'upon this – enterprise – and you look at the green trees and the sunshine on them, but you think of fogs, and ice, and storms, and voices, and fear and exhaustion, and it isn't easy to go. One doesn't have to be ashamed of it. You're frightened.'

'Yes.'

She remained still, and then gave a long sigh, as though she were very tired and had just made up her mind to lie down and sleep and forget about a world full of haunts.

'You'll go, though.'

When he spoke he had picked up the voice again of politeness and jokes.

'One terrible rule on boats. Washing-up before anything.' He was rinsing plates under the salt-water tap; the little kettle steamed domestically on the Buta ring. 'You sit quiet and embellish – you want to stay down here, or go up in the sunshine?' He was talking too much, embarrassed by his gauche words. Haunts . . . too ridiculous.

She stood up and walked about abruptly. Through the little portholes below the cabin's coach-roof one saw a little sea, a flash of sunny daylight on sparkling trees and water, but the view was barred by *Olivia*'s sturdy wooden deckrail. She spoke in a dull, wooden voice.

'I prefer to stay here for the present.'

She picked up the dishcloth and dried plates with slow circular gestures like someone killing time, waited till he had emptied the plastic basin and wiped round the tiny sink. He dried his hands and gave her a grin.

'Work's done – we can be as frivolous as we please. Where did I leave my cigarettes?'

'Frivolous . . .' Her face looked at him squarely with no smile; the black eyes bored at him. She pointed at the leather-covered settee. 'Is that where you sleep?'

'Yes,' a scrap surprised. Now she was pacing about again; what was the matter with the woman.

'I have things to say,' suddenly, 'but there are better ways of saying them.' She turned short on her heel. 'Undress me and put me down there.'

Most people have two sides to their head; Natalie, who came from Paris, had three. One thought 'Two little old idealists'. The second thought 'First time I've ever made love on the water – it's admirable. This is an unexpectedly good, patient lover, who knows what he is doing'. The third said 'Hurra – first worthwhile thing I've done in a year'.

She had different eyes, Raymond saw, when she made love. But she got her 'Paris eyes' back when she lit a cigarette. Realism had succeeded idealism. She was sizing him up, his body, his muscles, his proportions. He had to make an effort not to be abashed, shamefaced. He was conscious, as every man is after making love, of looking slightly ludicrous – but there is nothing so provincial as false shame. He looked steadily back at Natalie. A woman, after all, has more things to feel ludicrous about when she undresses – the silly line her brassière makes on her back, the even sillier ring round her waist from the elastic of her pants.

'Now I can breathe properly,' she said, smiling at him. 'Now, if you want me to be, I can be frivolous.'

He felt, he thought, rather wonderful.

'Be whatever you like. Whatever it is, I find it wonderful.'

'It is just that I've noticed that your boat is no place for a woman. I mean it isn't, obviously, anyway, at any time, but now especially. Women are lost without the bathroom. It was the great drawback to love in the eighteenth century. One had no worries about Gérard Philippe, but I've always been a bit dubious about Valmont – and as for Mertueil ... I think that what one does here is simply dive overboard. Do you think there's anybody there, on the shore?'

Raymond leaned across the settee and picked up his binoculars. 'We'll look' – climbing the two bottom steps of the companion. 'Can't see anybody. Nobody would get very excited round here anyhow – accustomed to sun-worshippers.' Just behind him, she gave his back a small amused kiss. I must be very careful, he thought, not to fall in love with this woman, or get sentimental about her. These games have Paris rules and provincial rules. I have to stay extremely detached. I could very easily find myself loving her.

He jumped up lightly on to the deck. 'I'll see what depth there is.' He sat on the rail, swung on his arms, and let himself drop feet first. He came straight up, wiping sea out of his eyes and nose. 'Metre and a half, about; you can dive.' The water was so clear it had looked as though *Olivia*'s keel rested on the bottom.

Natalie stood balanced on the rail in the diver's pose of recollection. She was not much tanned, and her skin was naturally brown, without absurd white patches. She looked fine. Raymond, paddling backwards, felt as proud as though she were his wife instead of heaven-knew-who's.

She dived, swam fast towards him, came up, and gave him a sudden wet kiss. Spontaneously, he grabbed her and kissed her back, with affection. She swam away neatly, her body graceful in the clear water.

'Cold. But good.'

'Comes from the mistral. Can't stay long.'

'I see I haven't thought how to get back on the damn boat. Is there a trick?' *Olivia*, her dead weight pushed by Natalie's spring, had turned her back primly and gone for a little walk all by herself. Her solid black side was high from the water, and awkward to scale.

'I'll go first, I know the trick. Now take my hands and get a foot against the wood.' The cool hard body was dripping in his arms, a very fine sensation. He admired her while she hunted for a towel in her beach-bag.

'Wonderfully quiet.'

'No wind in the bay. I can take her out on the motor, or I can tow her with the dinghy to the point. She'll catch the wind, there.'

'Tow her. I don't think I could bear the motor.'

'Hold the tiller straight, would you?'

'Listen,' said Natalie seriously; they were a hundred metres off the little red lighthouse on Porquerolles jetty. 'There's no point in setting the whole village into giggles. Is there anywhere on the shore where we wouldn't be gazed at?'

Raymond thought; a remark Christophe had once made came into his mind.

'There's a villa out on the point; people who're only here in summer. It has a pretty garden.' He explained, while watching the right moment to lower his mainsail. One did not make a mess of bringing a sailing boat to her mooring.

'Sounds perfect. Tomorrow morning?'

He leaned over with the boathook. 'Bring the tiller a bit to your right.' The hook clicked in the loop of the floating oilcan. 'Got her.'

'Till tomorrow.' She gave him a wink and got into the dinghy in a thoroughly ladylike way.

Natalie was a step in front of him; he could not quite follow; he could not predict anything. There was a complicated thread in the pattern that he could not trace or understand. She had not behaved simply as though this were an adventure.

It was tempting to train his binoculars on the little balcony, just visible over the trees of the waterfront garden. She would be there, having a shower, changing before going down, cool and self-possessed, to drink the apéritif. A sail and a swim, and making love on the water, were enough to give one a good appetite.

Chapter Seven

In the early days he had spent on Porquerolles he had gone out often with Christophe to fish. Christophe's fishing was not very serious, but there was a lot for Raymond to learn. Not only about the weather, the fish, the ground, the local difficulties and peculiarities; about the country, the coast, the island, as well. Christophe's wonderful stories, full of comic phrases in picturesque salty French. They added, for Raymond, a third dimension to Porquerolles, a fantasy texture, a fairy-tale world. To the northerner, the island became a place where remarkable things had happened and would happen again. Possibly even to him. A little like Natalie, he could never quite rid himself of a sensation of unreality on this island. At any moment, he might find himself in a fairy-tale. Really, Christophe was to blame for Raymond's falling in love with Natalie.

'I had a customer,' Christophe had said, squatting comfortably on the engine hatch of the untidy fishing boat, 'who used to come out with me for the nets, like you. He was interested in history – everything was history for him. He used to point to all the forts along the coast and tell me about them. "Look, Christophe: that one – time of Vauban. That one – Crimea. Up there, where the semaphore is now – built by the Emperor. And that – aha, castle of the Saracens, Christophe, castle of the Saracens." '

'What Saracens? Algerians? Pirates?'

Raymond had been steering, leg cocked up comfortably. Rumblebelly-bump, went the antiquated, rusty petrol motor. They steered close in under the rocks of the Cap des Mèdes, and Christophe flung the cork floater, a ragged palm branch stuck in it as marker, over the edge and began to pay the net out in a long zigzagging curve.

'How do I know where they came from? For hundreds of years there were Saracens here, invading Provence. They had castles in the Maures, in the Estérel; they plundered the whole land. Oh canaille de sort, there is a great hole.'

The villa on the point was, sure enough, built upon the remains of some fort or battery. The garden was terraced inside ancient ramparts now overgrown with moss and myrtles, and inside there had been a blockhouse. It was probably Napoleonic in origin – had not the frigate *Amelia* dodged for months in the Passe 'the eyes of Lord Nelson's fleet'? – but to Raymond it was the castle of the Saracens, enshrined in a story of Christophe's.

'The major lived there then. He was a man. Big – big like three grenadiers and a quartermaster. Two metres high, weighing a hundred and fifteen kilos. I was a little boy then, eight years old maybe, bare feet. One day, I had to come to his house, he told me. I had to turn the handle of the gramophone – you know, such an old one with a big curly horn. "You stay there," he said, "and wind the gramophone, and you shall have some money, and a big piece of tart and a glass of porto. But you must stay behind the curtain, and you must not look out."'

A dramatic pause, which Christophe excelled at.

'And did you look?'

'Of course I looked.'

'And?'

'He was dancing. All by himself, in the moonlight on the terrace, to the music of the gramophone. Altogether naked, with a big mug, full of champagne. He was a fine sight, I tell you, a splendid sight. Ah, he was superb, the major,' with a deep loving chuckle. 'How he could drink – ah, how he could drink.'

That ugly villa with its strange overgrown terraces was for Raymond altogether enchanted from that moment. A castle of the Saracens, and a gigantic drunken shadow, solemnly waltzing alone in the moonlight to a rusty gramophone, with sharp little French eyes peering behind a dusty curtain.

The mistral was still breathing over the Petite Passe next

morning, faint but determined. Raymond had been out early in the dinghy to haul in his net, which had nothing in it worth keeping. He pulled the dinghy up on to the pocket handkerchief of beach at the head of the inlet, below the rocks of the point. Nobody would see it there. He climbed the worn steps of crumbling eroded old stone to the ramparts, disturbing three blackbirds and a grass-snake. Nobody came in this direction. Christophe was the caretaker of the villa, and he had once told Raymond that it was a place where one could be assured of quiet. Fluttering between the myrtles was a butterfly, sulphur-yellow, the underside of its wings two shades of soft clear leaf-green. In the ragged garden were agaves and aloes and a sort of wild hollyhock. Bits of it had an English look, with rambler roses falling off a tumbledown pergola.

He had an old rug, and boat cushions, faded and stained with sea-water, to lay on the grass-grown stones where the sun shone in a pool of silence. Dragon-flies were darting about over the 'garrigue', the tangled Provençal undergrowth outside the garden, and green lizards sat under it, enjoying the splinters of sunlight that penetrated.

Natalie, in a cotton beach dress, was sitting the other side of the rocky point, looking out to sea, where a cruiser and three attendant destroyers out of Toulon were practising minesweeping or some such pointless naval manoeuvre. She wore her big cheap straw hat, and had left behind the big Parisian sunglasses.

They passed the whole golden day there. They swam off the point, gingerly because of underwater rocks. They drank white wine that had been buried at the water's edge to get it cool. After eating they fell asleep, a real siesta in the faint dappled shade of a ragged fig-tree. Raymond forgot all about Valparaiso, the Corsican, the patch on *Olivia*'s hull. A plane, an army jet trainer, sailing in low on the final leg of its approach to Hyères airport, saw them there. The pilot was amused by Natalie, who was lying naked on her front with the hat over her neck, and circled back again to wiggle his wings at her, but she did not wake. When they did wake, they made love and ate chocolate. The leaves of the bushes rustled faintly, but neither the major nor the Saracens came to disturb them.

*

But at six in the evening – Natalie was lying on a tilted canvas chair in the little waterfront garden, soaked in the sloped westering sunshine – there was a faint shadow on her, on her peace. The mistral had died out utterly, and a smooth golden carpet lay on the path across the Petite Passe towards Giens in the west. *Sparrowhawk*, with the evening mail and freight and a handful of returning trippers, had faded out of sight, but one could still hear the faint murmur of her engines travelling lazily along the water, sounding softly in her ear. When it died at last she wondered if it had passed the bound of hearing, or whether the boat was lying by now at her mooring in Giens. The last distillation of the day's warmth was seeping pleasantly into her; she had passed a careless, lazy, childish day and was now wearing clean clothes. Like a child, she thought, that comes home sticky and happy from a party. It gets its face washed, and its mother tells it to play outside for an hour before supper. I am that child.

She should by all accounts have felt peaceful, and she did not.

It was no kind of remorse. She was ruthless with her love affairs. She did not save them up, or dribble them out economically. She gave generously, and cut courageously.

She was even sure, considering her actions with detachment, that this was not just a selfish moment of sensuality. It had some value after all. Not that she had a sentimental notion of consoling solitary and forlorn young men – she smiled rather to herself at the phrase – but she might, possibly, be able to give a tiny scrap of courage. When he went, now, perhaps the memory she would leave him might help a scrap, once it came to facing the ghosts among the mists, and the sinister powdery snow trembling down in dead terrible stillness, and the sudden squall. She had tried to understand.

'How strong is the wind?' she had asked, trying to understand.

He had pointed to the shrouds, the taut wire stays that hold the mast rigid.

'You see, they're held with a special cord, a lanyard, that allows extra give if there's unusual sudden strain. Under, they're fastened with special deep screws. These squalls – they can strip those screws right out of the wood.'

To face that, he needed an extra gram of fortitude. Perhaps she could not give it him. But she was going to try. He was doing a thing that few people saw a need of. It was sufficiently rare to be honoured.

Would he do that thing?

Since he had thought of it, yes – if he wanted to. Want, want, what a word. If he wished, if he determined, if he would count no cost. Count no cost – that is a good phrase, she thought. An excellent phrase.

Natalie, with one of the sides of her head, was looking lazily, happily out over the harbour. With another, she was determined to love, to give – and was happy about it. With another, she was wondering calmly whether it were barely possible that she was being taken for a ride.

She had not moved for ten years in the cinema world without having met would-be bloodsuckers. Miraculous inventions that just need a scrap of capital are common everywhere. But the cinema tows along a vast and colourful fringe of splendid talents hidden by the jealousy of producers, of superb if unwritten screen-plays, visual slants and camera angles that will astonish the world given that little break that only costs ten thousand francs. And the young men with smooth suits and smooth manners who describe themselves as publicity agents are always to be found in smart bars, and know all the photographers.

Were Raymond's manners a scrap too good?

She was a fairly well-known actress, fairly rich – and with, she suspected, a reputation for suddenly, spontaneously, losing her head.

Wishing to dispel disagreeable recollections, Natalie got up and walked through the kitchen into the bar. She had her dark glasses on again, and showed an interest in the rouget she would get to eat that evening.

Lot of fish there were, to be sure. The sea was full of them. Varieties one had never heard of were commonplace here. Who in Paris had heard of the white rascasse, the tour-de-rau? Most of them were no beauties either. If one went by appearances, one would never eat fish here. And one would miss the best thing on the coast. Difficult, wasn't it?

She drank the local Porquerolles wine, and had an apple after her spinach. She would go for a walk along the jetty; it was the classic thing after dinner. The cool sea air at night was perfect after the spinach, of which she had eaten too much, rather greedily.

From the end of the jetty, the island was a dark shapeless mass, lit only by the loom of the lighthouse. The frogs were quacking madly back there; one could hear them even above the rustle of the quiet sea. There was a boat out too somewhere with a puttering breathless motor, sounding all the time as though about to expire but struggling on somehow. A passenger plane droned lazily over towards Marseilles; she saw first the green, then the red sidelight, and then the winkers beginning as it lost height and speed with careless confidence, knowing exactly where it was, what it was doing.

As she started slowly to walk back along the jetty, along the lines of moored boats, their night sound struck her. The soft lipping of the bows to the water, the soft creak of gear and the tiny rubbing bump of wood against moored wood. The dearest sound there is, to anyone that has ever been to sea in a small boat. Suddenly a voice spoke out of the darkness, startling her horribly.

Raymond had been sitting on the coaming of the cockpit, listening as well to the sound of the Mediterranean night. His eyes, accustomed to the dark, had seen her stroll, absorbed and thoughtful, along the jetty; he had felt that it would be unbearable not to speak to her, to touch her, to try to show her that he loved her. He loved her. There was not the slightest thought in his mind of any advantage to be gained. Love had distilled that. He wanted nothing but to be near her, to breathe the same air. Sharing, with her, the island of Porquerolles was giving him an immense happiness. On a sudden impulse he had pulled in the dinghy painter, stepped in quietly, and cast it off.

'You gave me a fright.'

'Come down into the boat,' he repeated. She hesitated for a long moment, looking back at the reassuring vulgarity of the lights of Hyères over on the mainland, then stepped down into the darkness; dazzled, she could scarcely make out the shape of the dinghy. With an oar, Raymond pushed off gently and used his hand to slide along a moored boat. The rustle and ripple of the water intoxicated Natalie. The sound of the boats had been so gentle, so reassuring. Raymond only had to glance over his shoulder to steer accurately for his riding light.

It had been cold on the water; the little cabin was warmed by the oil-lamp, but she shivered violently in her frock.

'You're chilled. I'll cover you with a blanket.'

'Like a redskin. Your hands are cold; come under here with me, then.'

'You want me very much, don't you?'

'Yes.'

'I understand. You're shivering like mad. Make yourself less tense.'

'When the snow starts, my body won't be there to provide warmth.'

It jarred on him; nothing had been further from his thoughts.

'No. I suppose not. I have plenty of solid warm clothes. I thought about it carefully. And I am from the north, you know. We understand cold, there.' He spoke lightly, summarily, as though he wanted to dismiss the subject, but she persisted.

'Did you come all that way – with the boat?'

'No. But I've been round France and Spain, in England, Ireland. On cruises, calling at ports, sleeping in harbour most nights. Not like the Atlantic. But it's much more difficult. Crowded waters, narrow, and dangerous. Steamer paths. Tides. Lights everywhere – tricky to navigate. On those west coasts in the narrow waters a gale is as violent as in mid-Atlantic, and a lot more dangerous. From the point of view of danger, I've done much worse things than this.'

It sounded slightly defensive, she thought.

'It's the distance that's impressive,' she murmured. 'It's a very long way.'

'Yes.'

Her voice gathered strength suddenly.

'What will you do when you get there?'

The tone was not hostile, but he felt a certain challenge in it.

It irritated him. Women – what did they know? It was his business; she had no affair asking such questions. Women...

He had no answer ready; he did not know himself.

It was a thing that had never seriously occurred to him. He had thought, sometimes, of all the jobs he had done, and had had vague visions of something similar perhaps, but grander. The humiliations would have been wiped out. There would be plenty of people willing – no, enthusiastic – to offer him any number of interesting positions. He had, after all, brought a small boat from Europe single-handed. Round the Horn too, not through the Canal. And very likely nearly left his skin there, too. But he had not thought about it. He had to get there first.

'I've done a lot of things in my time,' he muttered, a little irritably. 'I won't exactly be flummoxed.'

It reassured Natalie. If he were a fake, she had thought, he would surely have a glib enough tale. He would be full of schemes for publicity, for sounding trumpets on the sides of two oceans. But, she judged from that rather shamefaced mutter, he hadn't thought about it at all. As though the gesture had no importance to anybody but himself. And that, surely, was what gave it value.

Was Raymond's vanity – that of simple self-absorption – any worse than that of the cinema hanger-on, with his almost innocent, touching faith in the power of publicity?

Natalie knew just how much faith to put in publicity, but it had its uses. She was thinking, a little sadly, of the disinterest a country can show. The mentality of 'Just as good as the credits of your last film'. How big did you get your name printed, last time?

But a strange continent, where even the speed of the submarine cable – or, come to that, the radio-relay satellite – does not take away the feeling that Europe is a long way away to be sure, and pretty unimportant too ... Would anybody care a damn about Raymond or what he had done?

Did it really matter? The important thing was that he should do. That was what mattered to him – and who cared about everybody else? It mattered to her too, now.

Raymond was still feeling jarred, as though he were being

hustled. He would think of all that when it was advanced so far. There was so much that was more important. Women thought it was simply a matter of picking a name out on the map. A pretty name, preferably. And then packing one's bag and going.

Natalie now – she was looking around his cabin, the way she had, fixing it all in her mind. What could she know about his long evenings? – the charts and maps bought with pain, sweated for. The wearisome days in libraries, the books borrowed from as far away as Aix. The notebooks filled with tedious data about winds, tides, rainfall, temperature, sea currents. The coasts. The fish. The entirely new stars in the southern sky. The weeks of anxious thought about the route, with its possible stopping places, its possible alternatives.

It had taken him a year already, all this. And he was not yet ready – she could not know that there were still a thousand tiny details that needed studying, verifying, before he could feel that he had armed himself as well as could be against the unknown. That what remained, now, was a question of courage, of character, of fortitude.

All she was thinking of was what will you do when you get there . . . He had to get there, first.

He wanted to break the long oppressive silence, but what good would it do to tell her that they were on different boats? He was grateful to her, he appreciated her. Damn it, he loved her, and she had seen that, understood that. But she wanted to understand more – and he didn't want to be understood. He wanted to be loved. Oh, women. Can't they leave a man's mind alone?

What was the matter with him, now – that was a thing only another seaman would understand. A seaman under sail, not a cowboy in a liner. He was a seaman. He had taught himself, painfully, the things a seaman knew and understood. He knew he was a good officer. The bookwork, the currents, and stars, the technical knowledge. The judgement and control and anticipation. That was his; he was secure, confident.

But was he a good seaman?

Could he, as he knew he would have to, face a snowstorm, gale force, zero visibility? In that, could he go forward to serve a sail, with his little fish-hooks frozen? In that, what would he do if – it was a recurrent nightmare – a block jammed at the top of the mast, so that he could not get the sail down? The throat halyard block – he could see it in front of him. Getting up the mast was a horror to him even in a calm.

He had done everything he could think of; the mast was sound, the rigging without flaw, the blocks large enough, strong enough, smooth enough. The wringing strain – of the gaff on the mast, that has crippled many boats – was minimized. But who knew what the South Atlantic was keeping for him?

He turned suddenly to Natalie and clenched his hands together behind her back.

'You don't know what there is, that I worry about,' he muttered confusedly. 'The mast, the sails. You don't know what wind can do . . . Just don't despise me.'

'Of course I don't despise you. I am here to help. You will beat all that. They all said the Eiffel Tower would fall down too – it's still there.'

She heard the sigh he gave as she turned her body to hold him and rest him. Was it the sigh of a man who has accepted, finally, every risk, every danger, and accepts too that there is now nothing left to do but to go on, since it is now too late to turn? Or was it the sigh of giving up, of turning to a woman for oblivion, ease, peace? She didn't know.

She had to know, somehow. She had gambled on the throw of this dice. What? Not her virtue – oh really, her virtue . . . Nor her reputation. What was that? – something she kept for cameras. Faith, perhaps? What was love but faith? She too had to have something to believe in – Valparaiso was as good as anything she had ever found. She wished desperately to know. She knew that she must keep silent, especially now, that she had talked too much, would always talk too much. But it was so desperately important for her that he should go. He could not possibly know that. She had to ask one more question. Just this one last question. Knowing that she was a fool, that he would be furious.

'When is the time – the best time – to go?'

He pushed out of her arms and got up abruptly. He walked

up and down, fiddled with the wick of the lamp, picked up a cigarette, and put it down again. They both knew that he was hating it but that he had to give the answer – the true answer.

'Now,' he said.

Chapter Eight

It was not even true. He should have left weeks before. To keep to the schedule of winds and currents, he should have been in the Canaries by now, fitted, provisioned, poised for the big jump. June off Cape Horn was appalling, but all the other months were even worse.

But it would still be possible. If he left now, today. Only just. After a week it would be – once again – a question of next year. And he could not leave in a week. A shipwright could not fit *Olivia* with half a new hull in a week if he began this minute – and if Raymond had the money to pay for it. And the weathervane sail that was still not quite right, the stores incomplete, the rigging still not entirely above suspicion – he was not proud of that bobstay . . .

But he had had to say it; the truth had been as it were screwed out of him. If he had not loved her, he would not have needed to say it.

Absorbed in the joys of love, he had thought of telephoning Jo, to say he was not coming over to Saint-Tropez. Now, he felt that it was a heaven-sent excuse for running away slightly. Not that he was scared – but he did not feel very happy at facing Natalie for a day or so. Not that he had admitted that, this week once gone by, it would be a year again to wait. She did not know that. Not that . . . oh hell. He would go to Saint-Trop. He needed a change of scene, a change of company. It would give him new ideas. Mm, there was a light wind, on his beam on that course. Mm, Saint-Trop is eighty kilometres odd by road from Hyères. More than fifty sea miles, round Cap Camarat and the great mountainous mass of the Maures. Fifteen, eighteen hours sailing – if he went now he would be there early tomorrow, and could have a good sleep before the Corse turned up.

He looked across the sunshine – it had that fresh early-morning look about it – to the waterfront. Natalie would still be in bed; there was no risk of meeting her there. He would go and buy bread, and some meat for a change – he had set no net the night before – and make a pot-au-feu on the paraffin stove, nice and slow; there would be enough for three days, with potatoes, and lots of vegetables. Directly he was back he would let his mainsail draw – a nice comfortable sail. He was looking forward to it.

Once well out to sea, with the haze clearing, he picked up his binoculars to get a bearing. Yes, he could just pick up Cap Bénat there behind the jut of Port-Cros. He looked at the compass – yes, nearly abreast of Le Lavandou already; who would have thought it? *Olivia* was slipping along as well as ever she had done. The wind was steady, but very light. Of course, she sailed better now that the bottom had been scraped and repainted.

But that reminded him again of the wound, the great gaping rotted wound that had destroyed his whole existence, that was poisoning him, eating into him. He would not think about it. It was a lovely day, a fine day for a sail.

He thought, as he had sometimes, about a square-sail. But the yard was a pest. He intended to run before the trade wind with two staysails, guyed out at each side. She would be steady as a train, so. That was a sea-boat for you. He remembered – it was his greatest pride – the three-day gale off Belle-Isle. He had ridden it out in open sea, with a huge sea-anchor and a spitfire jib for riding-sail. He had had no more cares than the longing for coffee.

There you are again – he would never dare risk being caught at sea in a blow, now.

If he could get a bit of good old wood worked into her hull he would go bail for the rudder and the mainmast – she was sound above water, throughout. He would still show them what he could do. What she could do. Whatever he did, or didn't, the boat did the work, made the passage. A good boat . . . women were only women after all.

When he got back, he would have to tell Natalie. It was the only way. He would have to admit that he could not go because the hull was rotten, because he could not pay to get it mended. Why not tell her, anyway? It was only vanity that he had not told her. Come to that, admit it straight out.

He knew all the same why he had not told her. He was afraid that she would look at him squarely and say 'Why don't you work for it, then?' She was direct enough.

But she loved him; she had told him. She didn't mind his being poor. She would understand. And she had lots of money – the thought travelled like a comet – she would give him the money. He was certain of it; the more he thought of it the surer he was. When she had understood, she would give him the money he needed for the repairs, for the last tests. And then, next year, he could really go. This summer, final trials on the sails – a whole season to perfect the weathervane. A real shakedown cruise – round Corsica say, and down to Lipari – to give a thorough, prolonged test to the new hull. Get his navigation really back on the top line; he hadn't taken a star-sight in a year. Get all the stores built up. Yes, next March he could go. He would be free then of this miserable country, that miserable bank. Taxes, the scraping poverty, the endless ironic, cynical eyes – good-bye all.

And perhaps – who knew? – weeks more, months more, with this magnificent woman. She loved him; it was enough.

Natalie looked at the harbour, suddenly missing *Olivia*, the small silhouette, blunt and black, that had become both dear and familiar in only two days. Odd. Eleven in the morning, not back from fishing yet? Not possible, now that she thought – had he not said, last night, that he had sunk no net?

Could he be gone? She had asked him a bitter question; he had made a bitter answer. 'Now.' Had he made a slight drama out of that, and – literally now – left? Had he perhaps felt that she had pushed him too far, and pulled up stakes, in one spontaneous move: now or never, boy?

If that was so, it was a piquant history to add to her collection, she thought with irony. A forty-eight-hour love-affair – good heavens, just like a drink cure. She could stand on the shore, singing 'Mon Légionnaire' with a pathetic catch in the voice.

She had come to this island on a whim, stayed for a couple of weeks' peace and quiet to get over three months' nervous exhaustion – a nasty film, made under exceptional difficulties on location, in the depressing surroundings of the Belgian border. It had poured with rain the whole time, everybody had snapped everybody else's head off, the twenty-three-year-old, spoiled, neurotic little star had run away back to Paris twice after throwing tantrums, the director had caught a streaming cold on top of his treatment for benzedrine addiction, and Natalie had taken an overwhelming dislike to her screen husband – who had acted a mean, small-minded long-distance lorry driver with perfect realism throughout.

She had come here for as big a change as she could manage to find – and fallen straight into a fairy-tale. What was it about this island, where fairy-tales grew like the cabbages there in Arras?

There was Christophe over there on the jetty. He understood life here. He was the king of the fairy-tales; he told them to everybody, but was much too clever to live them. She wasn't angry with him on that account. Would she too make a fairy-tale for him to tell to visitors, like the Saracens and the major? The film-star and the sailor-boy. It would be a short story, but comic.

But Christophe didn't know it yet, unless she told him. Perhaps she would tell him – they spoke the same language; the black eyes and the green eyes understood each other.

He gave her his beaming smile, that comic mixture of gaiety and cunning.

'Caught any fish?'

'Kilo and a half. Nothing much worth having. A little bouillabaisse – all small fry.'

'What are you doing this morning?'

'I'm going to the beach, to inspect my little cabin where I sell drinks to tourists in summer. Have you seen that? That would amuse you? You like to walk with me then? The women will all be furious. They will say "That Christophe – thinks himself now a second Raimu. Does he now imagine himself beautiful, playing the gallant with Madame Servaz!"'

'We make a charming couple. Yes, I'll walk with you, it amuses me very much.'

'I have all sorts of exciting things in the cabin – potato crisps, whisky, even an old mattress. Bit mouldy, mind.'

'I can hardly wait.'

They walked through the village together, Christophe waving at everybody he saw like the President of the Republic.

'So, Madame. You are liking Porquerolles?'

'It's not a difficult place to like.'

'Sometimes people get bored. There is nothing to do but fish, or sail. Or drink, of course. People need amusement.' The malicious green eyes were clear and innocent.

'Men fish,' she said. 'Not being professionals, they never catch anything. But they succeed in enjoying themselves. Women are much the same.'

'They like hunting. Alas, there is no game left on Porquerolles. A few pheasants, maybe.'

'I am quite content, myself. I haven't the hunter's instinct, to shoot at rabbits just because there are no tigers.'

'So one goes for a sail.'

'Yes. I had a pleasant sail a day or so ago. But I am strictly a calm-weather sailor.'

'There are people who come,' began Christophe in his storytelling voice, 'to fish, or to sail, or to do nothing – for a fortnight's rest, you know, like everybody – and they discover a new life, less troublesome than the old one. They like it so much they don't want to leave. It is nice for the very respectable ones – they can pretend to be disreputable here, and that does them a lot of good.'

'Travel will broaden their minds.'

'Travel can be dangerous sometimes. I have seen some sufficiently remarkable things. They do things they would never do at home.

'I didn't see Monsieur Capitaine in the harbour this morning.'

'I noticed he was missing. Gone for a sail, no doubt, though there isn't much wind. A little breeze.'

'I thought him rather nice. He has good manners.'

Christophe grinned.

'Yes, some boat skippers like to take women sailing and make little propositions. Our Monsieur Capitaine wouldn't do anything like that.'

She grinned back.

'Nevertheless I found him interesting company.'

'Yes he is an amusing fellow. A few cracks in the skull, and that is entertaining, non? He is a great boat fanatic. We, you know, we only bother that our boats won't sink while we're hauling the nets, but a yacht – an obsession. A bug which bites you. Men who have them can never stop playing with them.'

'It's a good boat he has there. I know nothing about them but I thought it very well arranged. One could do all sorts of things with a boat like that.'

'Aha. A lobster only needs his shell. Men need too many things altogether.'

'A lobster, though – he doesn't feel the same urge to see new places.'

'To cross the Atlantic, for instance.'

'So – you know about that, then?'

'You mean he told you? Peuchère, I would not have thought it.'

'It's my big blue eyes that inspire confidence.'

'The things men will tell women,' shaking his head gravely. 'He must be in love with you.'

'Perhaps; how nice. Don't worry, I shan't be horrid to him.'

'Did you believe it?'

'Strangely enough, I rather think I did. Do you?'

'I never know,' seriously. 'But mostly, to be truthful, I think no.'

'We will see which of us is right.'

'Here we are. You like a little glass of whisky?'

'Yes. Then I will make a little walk, perhaps out to the point.'

'You think he's gone? I mean really gone?'

'I've been wondering.'

Christophe roared with laughter.

'Have no fear – he'll be back this afternoon. Good appetite for your dinner.'

There now, thought Natalie, after she had walked half a kilometre farther, I forgot to ask him why he always wears bedroom slippers. Because he likes them, I guess; as good an answer as any.

Once again Natalie thought during her morning constitutional with different sides of her head. She could quite agree with Christophe, who took the view that Raymond was an amiable eccentric who spent his life pottering about his boat telling himself stories to make his life sound more important. But she could, equally, accept him as an idealist not yet conquered by disillusion, capable, still, of a gesture to the world that was not only defiance, that had a streak of the heroic.

And her third side – that which had allowed her quite calmly, quite deliberately, to prove to herself that she was capable of love...A sort of obscure hope stayed with her that day, but by next morning, when there was still no sign of *Olivia*, she had a feeling that was almost pride. Nobody had the faintest idea of Raymond's whereabouts; from the bar gossip it appeared that he had scarcely ever been over twenty-four hours away since coming to the island.

I am having absurdly childish feelings, she told herself; just like when one was a girl of fifteen and had taken a fancy to a racing driver, saying obscure furious prayers – oh God, please let him win. For him to go, to leave, to sail to Valparaiso, was not only important to her belief in an ideal, but to her love-affair. To her, a love-affair could only have value if she herself killed it, renounced it while she still clung to it, while it was still the centre of her life. Over the years, she had developed a sort of personal mystique about love. It was, to her, adultery: a sin. It had to be a sin; if it wasn't, sleeping with another man was a meaningless social pastime. 'The position is humiliating and the expense exorbitant', to paraphrase Lord Cheserfield. Something missing – yes, the pleasure is momentary. Consequently, to Natalie love without a sense of sin was a rather over-rated amusement. She could only redeem this sense of sin by punishing herself. Lovers had to have their heads chopped off while they were still precious to her.

She had formed this theory while still at the convent. She

89

could hear still the low melodious voice of the tall, the beautiful, the terrifying Mère Marie-Agathe. 'Mortal sin, my children, is not only a question of grave matter and full knowledge. It is the consent that counts. To accept and welcome a mortal sin with pleasure – that is what makes it terrible.' The consent had sunk into Natalie's mind as nothing else had. Her education had been a ragbag, stuffed full of totally useless facts about the battle of *Hernani* and Racine's alleged Jansenism; that Pascal and Voltaire were really very second-rate writers; and that French prose from Montaigne to Léon Bloy was stuffed with subversive and highly explosive individuals. Monsieur Combes might be too stupid to be antichrist, but Jules Ferry had been a greater disaster to France than twenty Bazaines. As for Christian doctrine, it was even worse, and Natalie felt that she was pardonably extremely vague about Christian modesty, the Assumption of the Virgin and the encyclicals of Pope Leo. But the consent stuck to her.

Never had she done anything that she knew or felt to be wicked without that fascinated horror at the acceptance of it. A passive pleasurable surrender was worthless; that wasn't a sin or anything else; it was just jelly-fishy. She had to make a voluntary step, a leap upon a sin, to catch hold of it and wind her arms round it. Directly she had heard about the voyage away from the world – away from sins and women – she had known she would take – had to take, so to speak – the step she had taken that day on Port-Cros. A step that was taken for the pleasure, she suspected occasionally, of taking another step away when the time came. Equally deliberate and – almost – equally delighted in, though that she only thought in unusually sardonic mood. The acceptance was worth nothing without the renunciation: that was her personal morality.

This time, the two had practically come together. It was ironic that the boat – instrument of bringing them together – should immediately be the instrument of their necessary, inevitable parting.

At moments like this she appreciated – no, she loved and valued – her husband. After the high crusading fervour of a grand renunciation, she generally had a reaction after coming back to earth. At these times, Fred was a tower. And when she got a telephone call to say that he was in Saint-Tropez on business and was it a pleasant idea if he came over and spent the weekend, she was delighted.

She was in the bar when the phone rang; when called she had only to move across to take the instrument.

'J'écoute ... it's you, Fred? ... How nice, where are you?' For a disagreeable moment, she had feared it might be Raymond.

'I made a killing,' came his voice, jovial. 'I'll tell you all about it if you like – I thought I'd come over for the weekend, or are you totally inaccessible?'

'Oh no. Monastic seclusion, but you're a strong swimmer. You go to Hyères, then drive out to a point called Giens and there you find a boat. What cunning trick have you been doing?'

'None really, just a couple of my Mediterranean artists have hit a winning vein – two lucky tickets for me.'

'Oh good. Bring a beach shirt.'

'I'll look. Those fearful ones with "Bonjour les copains" on the bosom?'

'All right, copain; be seeing you.' She felt gay. The idea of Fred, broad and solid, very 'Parisian', his manly bosom adorned with a cowboy shirt as worn by the 'Ye-ye' boys, made her giggle. She went back to her drink; Christophe was hanging on the bar and she waved to him. 'Bring it over here then. Raconte.'

'Ah, raconte,' amusedly. 'I have inspected my domain; all is in order. I have streamed my net; it is full of holes. You tell stories; you know good ones.'

'I know nothing exciting today. My husband is coming for the weekend, which gives me pleasure; there is aioli for dinner; the season for Atlantic voyages has begun.'

'Ah.'

'What then do you say about the disappearance?'

'Disappearance – oh, what a grandiose word. He's gone for a day maybe to Cannes or somewhere to see the girls.'

'It's possible. But just to amuse ourselves, shall we make a bet? Who pays the apéritif. Let's say – if he's not back by Monday.'

'Done,' delighted.

Natalie went off to eat her dinner, looking forward to seeing Fred. She was sure that Raymond was gone. And Fred was always especially nice after she had done something silly. What was the word – fantasies? Escapades? Did he always know for certain, or did he merely suspect? Fred was a good business man, quite intelligent – she never knew quite how intelligent. Whether he knew or not, it did not alter his attitude. He denied, tacitly, that his wife would ever think of going to bed with another man. No jealousy or spitefulness slipped into his words or actions at these times. Fred could no doubt be very tiresome, but Natalie felt a strong loyalty towards him. She would never do him a serious injury, or be the cause of an injury being done. Many lovers who had inclined to take Fred over-lightly had been chopped very suddenly.

Chapter Nine

With the light, variable winds *Olivia* made slow progress, and it had taken Raymond nearly fifteen hours' sailing to reach Saint-Tropez. Fred, going the other way in a rather nice crimson DS coupé, had taken one – like the Corsican, he was a tomahawk in an auto. The little harbour was pretty, not yet poisoned by the noise and the squash of the high season. There were plenty of moorings belonging to yachts not yet even in the water; he picked a nice one and tidied up leisurely. He spread his awning, stowed his sails, and went ashore for something to eat and a pleasant stroll. He felt calm and balanced; he felt sure that he had seen the way out of his difficulties. When he got back on board he went contentedly to bed for a little sleep before the evening.

'Hola. Hola, Ramon.' A flat hand was banging on the hull. 'Asleep, the lazy bugger.'

Light muscular feet thudded on the deck; a pair of expensive sandals appeared on the steps of the companion, followed by familiar trousers, tight and faded, followed by the Corsican. Raymond stretched lazily. The inevitable beach-bag was dumped on the table by his bed and a hand ruffled his hair.

'Bonjour, Admiral.'

A pair of legs had appeared now, which he looked at with pleasure; brown, smooth and luscious. White sharkskin shorts, a bare stomach, a comic brief shirt, cherry red, of some velvety material that only just managed to cover exuberant breasts. A thick plait of bronze hair and huge blue eyes appeared. Two sleepy smiles crossed appreciatively. The beautiful Dominique, la bella iocchi.

'You see?' the Corsican was saying with complacency. 'I always keep my word. There is the Karina for you and here am I, with lots of whisky and a pocketful of Vin's money. He is totally blinded by love.'

'What a beautiful sensation for both of you.'

'Yes, isn't it?' delighted by this perspicacity.

Last, rather shyly, appeared a small thin girl, a very pale blonde with brown eyes, who was dressed in a blue shirt and jeans – like a rather sweet miniature Corsican. She was very pretty, with tiny fragile hands.

'My Patricia I present to you, my English lily of the valley. This is Ramon, as you see, a good friend, a comrade. As you also see, citizen of substance, captain of a ship.' The Corse had all the inborn respect for a shipowner. He had never dreamed of questioning Raymond's character and abilities.

Raymond dressed – a wonderful shirt came out of the beach-bag with two bottles of Highland Cream – and they went on shore. To show off to the admiring parasites in Saint-Trop, drinking apéritifs on a terrace, with panache and outstretched legs, and then to make a nice drive across the bay to Sainte-Maxime in the famous sport auto, for a good dinner.

Raymond enjoyed himself greatly. It was a very pleasant change, being lordly on the coast. To eat expensive food in a hushed silky restaurant, to drink a good deal, to exchange slow cunning smiles with the magnificent Dominique. To laugh at the Corse's highly coloured tales of adventure in Cannes, to admire the simple, rather touching, very obvious adoration of the lily for him. To hear voices and music, jokes and gossip, to exchange reminiscences, sniffling affectionately at the vulgar lights and noise. To feel part of the band, that he belonged, was accepted, even greatly admired.

He got into a happy, careless, slightly drunk, devil-take-the-slowest mood. It did not humiliate him that the Corse paid for everything, that he rode in the little auto with the Corse driving; he had often staked Jo to drinks and food in penniless days. But he did feel a slight need to assert himself, to show these girls that he was not only the brains behind all this, but that he was no poverty-stricken beachcomber either.

He kept himself easily in hand till they got back to the boat and started drinking whisky. On his own boat, where he had no need to display his vanity, Raymond opened his mouth too far. It was very silly; he even thought so at the time. They all gave admiration to the way he had his life arranged. It was comfort – it was even luxury to them, who had lived their whole lives in untidy sordid rooms. And this boat – it moves, it sails, it can go anywhere. The handiness of everything and the mobility of the whole brought naïve wonder from the girls. The Corsican had a superior smile at this; he knew all about boats now; damn it, he lived on one himself. Of course, the girls had never been aboard it – that would never do.

'Sure,' said Raymond, grinning at Dominique's silly, generous mouth. 'It can go anywhere I want it to. Across the Atlantic if I please. Might be an idea at that. Always wanted to have a look at South America.'

You fool, he was thinking, you idiot. But he could hear his own stupid voice going on, confidential and sly over the glasses.

'Not just yet, though. I have a rather pretty bit of business in hand. I have acquired a very promising woman – cinema actress,' casually. Really, he thought, you can get pretty low, can't you? It was too late for regrets.

'Who, who?' The bella iocchi, a great amateur of illustrated magazines, now all agog.

'You know Tatiana Laszlo?'

'Oh yes. Bit old – good, though. Terrific actress. Not her? Oooh.'

'She's at Porquerolles on holiday. We get on very well. I had her here on the boat, over in Port-Cros. Spot of sun-bathing.' He was filled with disgust at this lecherous hinting tone.

'Take any photos?' – the Corse, quite as impressed this time as the girls. A snap of an actress, preferably with her clothes up to her neck – worth money as well as lots of fun. The little Patricia was gazing round the cabin wide-eyed. Think – an actress had taken her clothes off in here.

'You with your crude ideas,' said Raymond, lordly. Such an idea too – with Natalie. Unthinkable, but not unspeakable. 'You know I don't go for that cheap stuff. A softer touch and a longer haul – pay more of a dividend in the long run.'

'Gold-mine there. Why not pass her on to me?'

'You're not quite in that league yet, my brave one – you stick to Americans,' very superior.

'Don't you dare sleep with any film stars,' said the lily fiercely.

'That sort of woman needs skilled handling. Still, if I think of any way you can get anything out of it, count on me. I haven't explored all the possibilities yet.'

'Any husband?'

'Man called Servaz – Parisian. Some sort of art-dealer. I've seen nothing of him – she's alone, so I've been passing her time for her.'

'Servaz? Art-dealer? But I know the fellow.'

'Impossible,' nettled.

'Yes, I tell you. That's to say I know about him. He has a business here in Saint-Trop, sells pictures and stuff. Must be the same. By the Annonciade; he has a woman to run the shop but he comes every month or so for a few days, from Paris.'

'How d'you know?' suspicious.

'Ach, you know the little César, who lives in a tent over by Pampelonne? The crazy one. He pretends he's a painter. Well, he sold some stuff to this fellow, got quite a good price considering it's tripe. He told me. The fellow buys some pictures from these crazy ones, and sells them to tourists. Big profit. More power to him, I say; wish I'd thought of it, good racket like that.'

Raymond gave him an evil look. What business had a Corsican peasant to know anything at all that concerned Natalie?

'I can find out more about him – Vin knows him, he's been in the shop. Bought some pictures – he's a fanatic about them. Not tripe by the little César, of course – somebody called Segonzac, some such name. Didn't half pay a price. He has them on the yacht.'

'Mm. It has nothing to do with her anyway. She makes plenty of money on her own account.'

'I'll say,' said Dominique, enviously.

Out in the fresh air, seeing the Corse and his lily off – they were going to drive back to Cannes – he felt the whisky shaking him. He controlled himself severely; he had been a bloody fool. The lily had drunk a lot, but seemed quite sober –

remarkable, tiny little thing like that. Still, she must have some muscle, to handle the Corse.

He checked the mooring and the riding light, automatically, and slung a bucket on a cord to the dinghy painter, to stop it bumping *Olivia*'s topside in case there was any wash. He looked with pleasure at the lights, and the humming life of the café still going on across the quay – he and Jo had had many a drink there in former days.

Down below, the bella iocchi had already taken off all her clothes, and was lying ripe and gleaming in the lamplight, a lazy smile on the pretty, stupid face, probably pretending she was a film-star. Her breath smelt of whisky but her body had an elastic youth and freshness, just as thrilling as Natalie's softer, more sophisticated body. But – perhaps he had drunk too much – it was of Natalie he had to think the second time, to avoid a fiasco.

Chapter Ten

Next morning was horrible. The cabin stank and so did his mouth. The beautiful Dominique lay naked and gorged like Messalina among slummy blankets; the flies had found a piece of forgotten fish and the fresh air was too full of sunshine. He got rid of her without trouble; she had to change as well as wash before going to work – she was a chambermaid in a large hotel. She scampered across the port, turning round to wave energetically, apparently quite unaffected by her half-bottle of whisky, and what he vaguely recalled had been a strenuous mating-game. He put on dark glasses; it was flat calm and he set the motor going to shift *Olivia* along. He had had a good time, but was in a hurry now to get back to Porquerolles, to Natalie. The motor bumped and thudded disagreeably inside his head; he took four aspirins and put up the awning, rather grateful that there was no wind for sailing.

He got into Porquerolles about seven in the evening, feeling a lot better, having read Dumas most of the way, and made a dinner off the lavish fragments of bread, salad, and sausage brought by the Corse. He went ashore after mooring. He wanted an apéritif, but most he wanted to see how a three-day absence had sharpened Natalie's reactions towards him.

She was in the bar, right enough, drinking Americano, very dressed up, for her. A man was with her too; a square handsome man, a bit bullish, looking negligent and Parisian in a summer suit of café-au-lait linen and American-looking open-work shoes, drinking whisky sours and chain-smoking filtertip Gitanes. She disregarded Raymond altogether; he might not have existed. He felt uncouth and unshaved, and took refuge behind the belote players, leaning over for familiar greetings in a loud aggressive voice.

'Hey, Christophe.'

'Why, why, look who's blown in. Where you been – Elba? Making a little training cruise?' perfidiously.

'No no, only business. Boat business, some things I needed. And an evening with some friends in Saint-Trop. Nice enough, but it's a relief to be back. Not enough wind for any serious sailing.' He was passing it off fairly well, he thought. 'Play the queen then, stupe.'

'Ah, talking of stupes. When they were dancing you weren't in the orchestra, that's for sure,' playing the queen. 'Since you point to her I have to play her now. Léon's waiting for that queen, as you might see if you knew how to play this game.'

Raymond was snubbed, and sat on a chair defensively.

'Never have learned how to play that damned game,' the man was saying. 'Anything more complicated than poker dice scatters my poor woolly wits.' He sounded sleepy and contented. 'My, I've absorbed enough sun to floodlight Versailles with.'

'You'll be grateful for it – sure to be pouring in Paris when you get back,' said Natalie. 'Stay there quiet and I'll get you another drink.'

So – that must be the husband, whom the Corse had seen in Saint-Trop. Raymond understood then why Natalie was being carefully distant – she was being tactful, of course. She was leaning over the bar in a wifely, comfortable way, then twisted her body to look at the belote players.

'Pastis for you, Christophe? I owe you one – I've just recalled.'

'Pardi, Madame. A big one – these cards are laughing at me. That spade knave, with his false slippery eye – peuchère, he thinks himself more clever than me.'

Natalie brought his drink across herself, and appeared to see Raymond for the first time.

'Ah, Monsieur Capitaine; good voyage? All the way to Saint-Trop? – my, that is a long way; a real passage, you might say.' Her voice was neutral, indifferent.

He imagined that it was a warning – 'look out, husband'. He was about to make a stupid answer when Fred interrupted.

'You've just come from Saint-Tropez – by sea? What, in a motor-boat?'

'No, sail, but I cheated and used the engine. No wind.'

'How long does that take, then?'

'About twelve hours – I left around six-thirty this morning.'

'Good grief; it took me an hour and a quarter by car and I hated every second – was it a relief when I found that ferryboat thing waiting there on the point.'

'Pity. If I'd known you could have come with me.'

'Here, why don't you sit here by us? – what are you drinking anyhow? I see you've met my wife so there's no need to introduce you. I'm Fred Servaz. You don't really like Saint-Trop, do you? I go there often on business, find it a misbegotten place.'

'Not particularly.' Raymond was recovering his assurance; it is always amusing to drink with a husband one happens to be cuckolding. 'It was just handy to meet some people I had to see on business.'

'So you're a yachtsman? Don't use any technical words – I don't know which is port and which is starboard.'

'I'll spare you,' laughing. 'But surely it's you, then, the owner of the picture-shop there – behind the Annonciade?'

'Quite right. My secret shame: I refuse to admit it in Paris. You see – tourists go to the Annonciade, to look at the Grammont collection, which makes their mouths water. My idea is to catch them going out. Of course, it's only a little shop, and not terribly serious. If I have a Van Dongen to sell, naturally, I do so in Paris. But I go there every month or so, because I have a little stable of local artists. My windows are full of course of stuff to catch the eye. Hand-painted copies of yachts by Dufy.' He was probably a bit drunk, but perhaps it was only the relaxed, friendly 'Porquerolles' atmosphere that was making him talkative.

'Ah, now I know. An acquaintance mentioned a local artist while I was there. Some boy called César – perhaps it means something to you?'

'Yes yes, certainly. There are tremendous lots of these locals who play with paint, you know, but every now and then one appeals to me and I buy – hoping it will appeal to the public. In point of fact it is generally a poor investment, but I do making a killing every now and then, now that abstracts are no longer fashionable. I hate abstracts – agreed most heartily with Georges Wildenstein. That boy César has quite a lot of talent; I've done well with him.'

'I have a feeling I've seen some things bought from you in Cannes, fairly recently. On a yacht – could that be possible?'

'On a yacht – ah, not my dear old Vincent? Friend of yours?' carefully casual.

'No,' laughing, 'not my kind of yachting, and I'm one of these extraordinary people that like girls.'

'That's him,' with a happy shout. 'Mark you, he's charming, and a great one for fine arts; I sold him a whole salon full of a most promising young man of mine. Signac and water, you know, but with a tempting freshness. You like pictures yourself?'

'Doesn't everybody?'

'Oh my boy, I wish they did. Still, I can't complain. You know, I had a sculptor on show last week; the most awful risk but I felt quite strongly about him. And a miracle happened: I've sold the bloody lot and got some famous prices. He's terribly happy too, because I hadn't paid him anything to write home about – too much risk of being left with the lot, holding the baby, huh? But I've got him a promise of a show in Amsterdam, and if he clicks there I have first option on him in Paris; cunning, you see.'

Natalie was finding the situation an annoying one, but she could see a certain comedy in it. Dear Fred, she thought, being expansive and confidential in that way he has, so that anyone would think picture-dealing was child's play. Often people think him a fool, mistakenly. Telling all this ta-ta-ta to Raymond, who isn't understanding a word.

Raymond, however, was following with attention. Wasn't it a racket? And it was interesting to know about anybody's rackets.

'You buy stuff outright then? Instead of just taking a commission on sales?'

'That's the normal method. But here there are two factors. First is that these local people prefer hard cash in their hands to a possible wait of six months with nothing, very likely, at the end. Second, I cover my risks better. I gamble with them, after

all. I buy a picture for five pounds; maybe I sell it for fifty –
good, this week I did. But plenty of times I won't get ten bob.
Once they've had any success they're able to drive a harder
bargain – make no mistake,' with a grin. 'Forgive me, I have to
give Paris a ring before eating.'

Natalie was turning her glass round and round reflectively,
chewing her orange peel.

'Any chance of seeing you? I have a lot to tell you.'

She raised the black eyes to his face, and stayed a long time
silent, thinking.

'Yes,' she said at last. 'I can arrange that. About ten-thirty,
but I cannot be certain. At the castle of the Saracens,' with a
mocking, ironic emphasis on the last words.

Fred was coming back, puffing at his cigarette, humming the
tune the television was playing, off key.

'Arranged,' he said. 'I'm to see her on Monday and I'm to
bring the money. Tiresome old bitch. As though one couldn't
postdate a cheque as one does for anybody. But no – come in
person and bring money in notes. I ask you . . .'

'Extraordinary that people don't trust picture-dealers?'
Natalie was grinning, teasing him.

'Extraordinary that it's so often these dotty old women that
own valuable things,' said Fred, only half angry. 'Sorry,' to
Raymond. 'Boring for you to talk about business all the while.
Hell, I'm on holiday even if it is only a weekend.'

'It doesn't bore me at all. I'd like to hear if it isn't confidential or something.'

'Hell no, nothing confidential, just an example of how crazy
things can be. If you're really interested . . .' dubiously.

'Sure.'

'Well, this old woman in Saint-Cloud has something I want
– that is confidential, if you like – very expensive but genuine
fourteenth century and I have a buyer. So I went to see her last
week. She agreed but as you heard me mention she insisted on
cash payment. Which I didn't have – there's a considerable
sum at stake. Rather than borrow I decided to raise what wind
I could – luckily I've done well this week in Saint-Tropez. Now
I've got to dash up to Paris taking all the loot, pay in my
cheques immediately. You see my woman there pays them

into the bank in Saint-Trop and that takes a week. What a to-do.' He laughed. 'Let's eat.'

'Hope to see you before you leave,' said Raymond politely. 'But I should have thought she could take your cheque.'

'That's just it,' said Fred, grinning. 'Having it, vaguely, is one thing. Having it liquid, immediate, in actual cash, is a thing we're no longer accustomed to. Think if a customer came in and paid in gold dust, or raw diamonds – we'd be flummoxed. Still, I've made it, even if exhausted in the process. Bye – pleasure meeting you. Come on Natalie, I'm starving.'

'All very complicated,' said Natalie indifferently. She knew well that Fred was not annoyed. He enjoyed these hair-brained schemes immensely and would not have missed them for the world. To him, the gamble was all the fun. A system whereby he was as good as broke, according to his bank statements, but perfectly solid and solvent in reality, tickled him. His wealth seemed always to rest on a customer six months ahead. A challenge, like this one, was a thing he would have accepted even had he had no customer for the picture, she thought. To grind himself down, to adopt all sorts of ignoble pretexts to raise money – he must have been doing some hard selling there in Saint-Trop. Totally exhausted, he would then come, as now, for three days' complete flop in a deckchair, and then drive off towards some other wild scheme. She rather enjoyed it too; she could quite see the attraction. Business was so boring. He would have got hold of pictures by piracy if he could.

But oh, he could be boring, thought Natalie, eating soup. He was a bore after two days, and insufferable after three. He was a compulsive gambler, as boring on that account as a race-course punter. He always did this trick of talking to total strangers in bars about his next horse. Pictures to him meant, simply, gambling. Yes, he had great technical knowledge of pictures, and loved them. But the punter – the professional punter – had likewise a deep, involved knowledge of horses, and frequently loved them too, passionately.

She knew a well-known director who spent his every spare minute at Longchamps or Chantilly. Often he betted – and always his heaviest bets – on a horse simply because he liked its looks, like a housewife betting on a lucky name. Because, in short, he had fallen in love with it. 'It won't win,' he would say, 'but I don't care. It's such a beautiful animal. I must bet on it; I have to bet on it.' Fred was like that.

He even loved pictures the same way. Because they gave him, sometimes, this kind of pleasure, he accepted losses on them in the same deliberate manner. But he made up for these big bets by hedging. Amassing, with certainty, money on small bets; coldly and almost meanly. And, whatever he did, he talked about it all the time. He could never pass an evening thinking of a Mozart opera, or a good dinner, or making love, or being at sea in a small boat – he was always too busy money-grubbing and talking about it, with intolerable self-satisfaction. Natalie hated that tourist shoppie of his which he so exulted over; she knew it was for him nothing but a series of cruel, careful little bets on a minor track, made by a professional punter who is intent on working up his stake for the heavy bets, on the big horses.

'I think I'll go tomorrow evening,' he said suddenly, gazing with pleasure at a huge fish which the waitress was dissecting. 'I can drive overnight and be in Paris early. I've recalled that there's an auction at Drouot I don't want to miss.'

'In that case, you'd better go to bed early.'

'I was anyway; I'm nine-tenths asleep now. What you doing?'

'I'm going to have a walk; I always do – don't bother about me.'

'I won't be in any condition to,' said Fred, yawning hugely.

When Raymond worked the dinghy into the tiny inlet and climbed the rocky path she was standing there, with a cigarette between her lips, gazing over the water, hands in her trouser pockets. She turned when she saw him, but took out neither hands nor cigarette, looking very unapproachable. Raymond did not quite know what was the matter, but there, he reckoned, women were always slightly odd and it never did to ask them. He lit a cigarette too and came to stand by her silently.

'You know,' she said at last, 'it's a pity. One comes to an island that everybody has always said is very beautiful. One goes for a walk along the beach, expecting the sea to have thrown up curious and beautiful things, and one finds every square foot covered in rusty sardine-tins and rotten orange-peel.'

'You've been over by the barracks, perhaps. Those sailors – undisciplined set of pigs.'

'Luckily one knows that, and that it is a mistake to think anything will be beautiful just because it sounds so.'

She's been drinking too much, thought Raymond. Now she's feeling depressed. It's not important.

'One gets over it,' comfortably.

'Yes.' She threw away her cigarette in a high arc over the rocks.

'Salt water,' she went on in the same monotonous voice, 'is a wonderful disinfectant, I hear. Good reason for preferring the sea to the land. Well – you wanted to talk. I didn't come here to make love, but I'm in a good listening mood.'

'I went away,' abruptly, 'because I had something I didn't know how to say, which I haven't told you. I couldn't tell you about it before; you might have thought I was cadging. When I told you I was ready to go – it wasn't altogether true. So I went off for a couple of days because I didn't know how to face you; I had to try and screw myself up.'

'Well, go on. I've been suspecting something of the sort.'

'You see, a few days ago – the day you came, wasn't it – no, the day before – Christophe and I hauled the boat out to paint her hull. We found a big rotten patch in the planking. It didn't show. But it's dangerous. Any time at sea in a bit of a blow, pressure comes on the hull – it might give way suddenly. She'd just fill with water and sink, at a second's notice. I can't risk her on a passage.'

Natalie kept silence. Something that doesn't show but is there, she was thinking.

'I didn't want to tell you about this. Then I realized that when you asked me when was the best time to go, and I said now ... you were expecting me to go, and you would wonder why I hadn't. Do you see? I can't go out into the Atlantic with the boat in that state; it would be suicide.'

Natalie still kept her wooden silence; Raymond paced about nervously.

'I knew you'd understand. Thinking about it while I was away, I thought I was stupid not to tell you, because of course you'd see. It was just an unhappy accident – I didn't have any idea of it myself. It came as a bad shock to me, I can tell you.'

'And is there a way of repairing this?'

'Oh yes. I can't do it myself – one needs a boatyard. They'd have to cut out that whole section of the hull and replace it with good wood. It can be done. You pour a layer of concrete on the inside afterwards to seal the join. It's never perfect – for that you need a whole new hull – but it would be seaworthy.

'It costs an awful lot of money though. And that's just my trouble – I don't have any.'

Indeed, thought Natalie. I am now supposed to ask how much an awful lot would be, upon which I get the classic answer that of course to me it wouldn't seem like an awful lot. I wonder how much he's hoping to get. It's not a bad story – has the merit of originality; shows imaginative power. Nicely worded – carefully prepared of course. Maybe he's had practice smoothing it out.

Naturally, I am the perfect touch, she thought. Not only am I a film actress, therefore with plenty of the necessary, but I take my clothes off into the bargain. It's quite pretty. Having taken off my clothes, I then unstrap my cheque-book. If this kind of thing is done well, it only needs doing once or twice a year. He can probably make a good living.

One was horribly humiliated, but it had its amusing side, didn't it, now? She got amusement into her voice before she spoke.

'My husband would be interested in this. He sells pictures, as you know, and is regarded as good at it.'

Raymond had missed the bus.

'What? I don't get it.'

'He sells pictures and you sell voyages – really there's very little difference.' It was clear enough but a sort of obtuseness stopped him realizing. Her soft, professional voice was perfectly level. Natalie, full of self-scorn, self-contempt, had good self-control. She had started to stroll towards the path, but he kept pace with her. She had to find a good phrase, she thought.

Something that would choke him off efficiently. Having realized that the fish had not taken the bait, he might very easily fall back on blackmail.

'You're quite welcome, of course,' she went on in the same amused voice, 'to tell my husband that I've been in bed with you. You won't find him sympathetic. As for me, I'm quite ready to repeat everything. The islanders, for instance. I notice that they find you a slight joke, but if they heard your efforts to get money out of me they might think you a slight bastard as well. And I've no doubt that wherever you went it would be exactly the same. Why don't you creep twenty feet underground – and stay there?'

She went on walking; he didn't follow her. Words, she thought, are better than blunt instruments. While walking rapidly back towards the village she exerted all her force to keep her detachment, but before getting into bed she took a sleeping pill, a thing she scarcely ever did. It was an admission of defeat, just a little.

Chapter Eleven

Raymond stood still for quite a while, hearing nothing. At last he got into the dinghy, and rowed with automatic gestures back to *Olivia*. He felt shocked, but not more than mildly. It all seemed to have happened before – he was vague. He went to bed; he was tired, had been up late the night before, had had over twelve hours at sea, had drunk a good deal. Sleep would build up scar tissue in his mind. But it took a good while before sleep finally mastered painful burns.

It was pure coincidence of course that Natalie should have chosen that metaphor, that wording. She could not have known – or remembered, if she had ever known – that the captain uses those same words – the captain who conducts the court of inquiry and later drowns himself, nobody knows why – of *Lord Jim*.

He was slow and heavy next morning, dragging, weary, with no wish but to burrow again under blankets. It was the church bells that woke him. He had no net out, and nothing to eat, not even bread. He dragged his head back on to the pillow and dozed off again. All that morning he spent in the state where one never really knows if one is asleep, and dreaming, or awake and just imagining. Both disagreeable . . .

But he got up, finally, looked at Porquerolles with repulsion – it had its Sunday look, and the boats were disgorging crowds of Marseillais with all their wives and children – and decided that, wherever he wanted to be, it wasn't here.

It was flat calm still; he had to use the motor to get out of the harbour. And he had no reserves of fuel left; he would have to go to Giens for that. And it was Sunday – the church bells pursued him all across the water of the Passe: no supplies to be had today. He did not know what he wanted to do, and for lack of anything better went to Giens and got on the bus, which took him to Hyères. It was in Hyères, looking across the square through the windows of a little café with a pinball machine, that his thoughts, bitter and revengeful, suddenly crystallized into the idea of telephoning the Corsican.

In Porquerolles, one could not make a call without its being known. Even if one's own voice was not overheard by half the island, there was no automatic switchboard. Calls from the island would be remembered, noted, maybe even listened to. Here, there was no risk of that.

'That you, Dominique? Yes, I'm fine. Yes, lovely. But this is serious. I have a job for you, urgent, important. I want you to phone Jo. Go on trying till you get him. Tell him business, and worth trouble. Make sure he's understood. Tell him to pick me up with the auto – let's see, I'm in Hyères now – pick me up in Le Lavandou; Café du Phare. If you can't get him or there's any snag, phone me there in Lavandou about two hours from now. Got it? See you this evening – perhaps. You understand? Don't leave any messages, and don't say who you are till you've Jo on the wire and you're sure there's nobody listening. Don't mention my name till he's understood. All right, my girl? Ciao.'

Very well. And now the Corsican would see that he was able to carry out a plan as well as make it. He would show him. He would show that cinema bitch, too. In the big Berliet bus, hurtling round the corners of country roads with screams and long melancholy sighs from its air brakes, he swayed about and thought of details.

In the café he ordered mint tea; he did not want any alcohol. He knew he could count on the Corse. That was one person he could count on, anyway, through thick and thin. It was a good warm feeling. Many disadvantages Jo might have – but loyalty ... Wasn't that alone worth all the others? thought Raymond.

The Corse had a plain red sweater on. Nobody looked at either of them. Familiar types, anywhere on the coast.

'Where d'you leave the auto?'

'Not here. Up the other end of the village.'

'Good. This is something pretty good, I think, but we've got to work fast. If the job's to be done at all it's got to be done tonight. We mustn't lay any trail. Between here and Saint-Trop, we've got to borrow Dominique's scooter.'

'Ah. You got a line then on that picture-shop? I've been thinking of it all week. I guessed it was that when she rang. But how do you know?'

'He told me. Simple as that.'

'But it'll point to you.'

'I don't see why. He was drunk, flapping his mouth through the whole bar. He's one of these types that has to tell every-body how clever they are. I'll bet there's fifty people who know all about it in Saint-Trop. We've just got to make it look like a local job.'

It suited the Corsican down to the ground. He did not tell Raymond, but he was in need of a bit of capital. Monsieur Vincent, as the local boys called the American ironically, had grown tight about money, and was becoming a little too urgent. He had decided to wrap up and vanish with whatever he had. He had been thinking that, if he had just a little capital, he would elope with the lovely Patricia. To Torino, perhaps, where he had relatives. With money, that could be made into a honeymoon in Portofino.

'How d'you know if it's any good, then?'

'There's money there. Takings for this week haven't been banked. The woman does it usually.'

'That's so. I've watched her take it to the bank in the evenings. I've had my eye on it too, but thought it was no good when she goes every day.'

'Well she hasn't – not this week. He wanted to raise all the ready money he could, for a big thing in Paris. He's planning to go on Monday, so the job's got to be done tonight.'

'I'd thought of having a go at her, but she sticks to the main street.'

'Even if half of it's in cheques there'd be something for us. It's probably in some bureau drawer – push-over if we can get in.'

'Getting in's easy with two,' said Jo with confidence. This was his department. 'I've studied the place, like I told you. Downstairs is hopeless – there's that steel trellis-work, and those special bolts on all the doors. But if we could get in upstairs there's a door down to the shop. And that has only a spring lock. And I think we could get in upstairs easy enough. There's an outhouse at the back and a wall. I've reckoned I could climb up there, if I had you to hold me.'

'What's upstairs, then? Draw the layout on a bit of paper – here.'

'We'd just need to be quiet,' said the Corse with confidence. 'There's only an old woman. Easy fixed. There's a man lives up at the top, but he works nights on the railway.'

'How do we get the old woman out? Can't we make a fake phone-call?'

'No phone. We'll fix her. I tell you I've studied it – it was just that I didn't think it worth anything. I've studied a dozen shops like that, but they're mostly too fly.'

'Now stop,' said Raymond. 'All right, but we've got to think this out carefully so that nothing can point to us. We've the time. Does anyone know where you are, first?'

'Dominique.'

'She's all right, as long as we don't tell her we're working there. Let her think the auto's panned, and that you need the scooter to get back to Cannes.'

'Write it all down, Ramon.'

'Dark clothes and tennis shoes – that's easy. Something for a mask, just in case, but we mustn't buy anything. I know – that bazaar on the waterfront; they have these carnival faces. Pick some nipper of seven or eight and send him to buy a couple.'

'We'll have to tie up the old woman.'

'No other way?'

'She'd wake up if there was any noise.'

'If we have to, then. You sure – really dead sure – there's no one else in the building?'

'Not a mouse. What else do we need? Write it down.'

'Ball of string. Cold chisel.'

'I've one in the auto. And a torch.'

'Hacksaw, in case there's a bolt. And an oilcan. Gloves – those housewives' rubber ones.'

The tourists had left on the evening boat, and the island was again quiet. Natalie and Fred had been for a long walk over on the south side of the island; she had not enjoyed herself very much. He had grumbled about his feet, and about running out of cigarettes. Great baby he could be sometimes. She had had a shower and changed, and felt fresh; he had fallen half asleep on his bed, saying he would be down for supper. She was glad of a respite from the irritation.

Automatically, she had strolled down to the harbour, as everybody always did. *Olivia* was missing, she saw at once. Aha, she wasn't going to believe he had left this time. He would be away grinding his teeth somewhere. Or simply shamed to face the possibility of seeing her. Or simply fishing, maybe. Or even decided to try another place where rich tourist women came along, to get maybe a hook into. She was detached about it now. It wasn't that bad.

It was a racket, to be sure, but was it any worse than Fred's? Was it even really a racket? Wasn't it at least just barely possible that it might be true?

Natalie was beginning to waver a little bit. She turned sharply and walked back.

'I'm putting off the evil hour as much as I can,' Fred was saying in a muffled voice between grunts; he was putting a shoe on, and the other lay under the bed nearly out of reach. 'I think I'd better go tonight all the same.'

'But you weren't planning to go till tomorrow, surely?'

'Ach, all this ferry affair, and then to get to Hyères, and from there to Saint-Trop – it all wastes too much time; I won't be in Paris till heaven knows when, and I won't be in Saint-Cloud till late evening anyway. I can drive all night, and have time tomorrow. But it's a nuisance – I'm enjoying myself.'

And you're a nuisance, thought Natalie. First this tedious uproar about a blasted picture, and now this stupid havering. Business men . . . pests, they are.

He was certainly behaving tiresomely; he dawdled over supper, and then drank a lot of brandy, and then drank large amounts of coffee to stop him falling asleep, and then his packing had to be done, and then no boatman could be found to take him to the mainland on a Sunday night, and bargaining had to be done; Fred slightly alcoholic and abominably cheerful, Natalie tired and curt. The boat skipper grumbled a good deal; it was after eleven when they finally pushed off. Natalie had waited dutifully at the harbour to see him off, still bonhomous and talkative, his beach shorts and a loop of flex from his razor sticking out of his bulging briefcase. She took it from him and repacked it neatly. He quieted the boatman's conscience with a good tip.

'Don't bother about that; hell, I'll throw it all in the car. Yes yes, I've plenty petrol. There's an all-night garage on the road anyway. Bye, my dear; see you whenever you're back in Paris.'

'Next week probably; I have to come up for a script.' She had been tempted the first day to go back with him, but rejected the notion. What reason had she to run away?

The boat buzzed off fussily into the darkness, Fred complaining that it was cold on the water. Natalie waved obediently and walked back towards bed, very tired, glad to be alone again. But directly she was alone her thoughts came buzzing back again like gnats.

Compare Raymond with Fred. Fred, let's say, is about fifty per cent honest. Maybe sixty. Not talking about legally honest. Morally honest. Fred does nothing legally dishonest, either. There is nothing illegal about selling virtually worthless works of art, generally faked in all but name, at prices anything up to a thousand per cent above what he had paid.

She was fond of Fred, just the same. She was married to him, and he was a good husband. Kind, loyal. He might irritate and bore her, but he didn't disgust her. Sometimes she even went to bed with him. Was Raymond any worse? What was there, genuinely, to get so indignant about? She had been so full of righteous indignation, of purple-phrased moralities. Just because her pride had been hurt. Just because she had been tempted by a wild idealist notion.

The notion was his, anyway. On lots of grounds, once she thought about it, he was preferable to Fred. He didn't talk about money the whole while. Come to that, he didn't even want much. He even preferred to be poor, dependent on nothing but his own wits. He didn't rub his nose in money, with his arms to the elbows in the dirty mess all day.

Would Fred ever have had an idea such as Raymond had had? Surely not. Such things never occurred to him.

Who cared whether Raymond did, in reality, ever get to Valparaiso? Whether, indeed, he ever seriously set out? Wasn't it enough that he had had the idea? Wasn't that, already, enough to show that he was further than ninety-nine per cent of human beings ever got?

Natalie was tempted to write a cheque for the money he had tried to get from her, to give it to him with no more than a touch of irony. To say: 'Here. I see through you, you see, but I find I admire you too, a little bit. This much: I think you deserve that.' And her days of happiness? Wasn't that, too, worth something? He had given her that, as well.

If she did that, it would be amusing to see whether he took it. Would he just take it, brazenly, calmly? Or would he redden, and refuse it angrily, and abuse her as she had abused him? He must want to get his own back on her somehow, in some way.

'I wish we'd had time to work this all out properly, all the same,' Raymond was saying thoughtfully. The bella iocchi had brought her scooter and obediently gone back on the bus. They would give her some money for that, if they made any. She might not have done it for the Corse, who had been faithless to her, for whom, indeed, she had wept bitter tears out of those beautiful eyes.

But she would do it, and twice over, happily, for Raymond. That was the man for her. She had never given herself with more joy, with more real happiness, than that night on the boat in Saint-Tropez harbour. Dominique was not a girl with any imagination, but she had always been struck by boats, with the anchored yachts swaying gently there above their fluttering reflections, ducking slightly to the faint lip of water from a passing dinghy, so lightly balanced they were upon the gleaming shot-silk water.

And at night: one did not see the dirty orange-peel and floating debris that fouled the harbour; the cast off contraceptive and dissolving cigarette packet. Nor the broken Coca-cola bottle, the empty rusty tin of aerosol-packed suntan and the cheap, broken dark glasses lying squalid on the harbour bottom. The water was clean, and so were the men on it.

'Qué, Ramon, not the slightest risk, I tell you. One old woman. It is a nuisance, but enfin, we tie her up; it is not difficult. The little street at the back has no café; it will be deserted at midnight. To climb is of a simplicity ... I only hope that what is inside is worth all this.'

'I just like to be sure, that's all. Jobs get ruined by thinking that a small detail has no importance. You can get pinched as easily for two ten-franc notes as you can for a million.'

Chapter Twelve

Natalie got up early and had her coffee in the kitchen instead of waiting for it to be brought to her. She thought while drinking it that if, by that remote chance, Raymond had spoken the truth about the boat, the one person who would surely know was Christophe. She walked down to the harbour. *Olivia* was still missing – where could he be? – but she was relieved to see that Christophe had just got in from hauling his net. He was sitting in his boat, disentangling fish from the tatty meshes; she strolled along the jetty, gave the warp a pull, and jumped as the boat's nose touched and began to fall slowly away again. Christophe looked up and grinned, and threw her a rag to wipe her hands, slimy from hauling on the sodden mooring warp.

'Bonjour, Madame.'

'Alors, raconte.'

'I have been asking myself where Monsieur Capitaine has been all yesterday.'

'I have a feeling that he has a grievance against me.' She sat on her heels on the engine hatch, watching the big sure hands that did not cut themselves on the spiny dorsal fin of a still-wriggling rascasse. 'Christophe, do you know whether there is anything wrong with that boat?'

'Like what? Whether it is a good boat? Not thinking of buying it, perhaps? I don't think he'd sell it.'

'No. I agree. It means too much to him. I hadn't thought of offering. I heard, just, that there was something wrong with the hull. I wondered whether it were true.'

'Do you think it might not be true?' The green eyes were full of amusement.

'I admit it did occur to me that it might be an invention – to get, let's say, money from rich stupid tourist women.'

'Ha.' He laughed heartily. 'What a good idea.' His face became serious again immediately.

'I do not think our friend would think of that.'

'So it's true?'

'Yes, it's true. I know because I discovered it myself a week ago, no more – pardi, the day you came. You were standing there on the harbour; we were painting. I tried the wood with my knife; there is a big rotten streak.'

'Is that dangerous? I mean, on a voyage.'

'Oh peuchère. The wood goes ripe like a pear – juicy, full of water. Ah, I begin to understand. He has been telling you all sorts of things. You have made a very deep impression, I can see. But that is not my business. The wood is tender, you understand. If there was a blow, the rotten wood does not bruise – but it might easily just fall apart. Like a bucket with the bottom rusted through.'

'I see. And that kind of a blow ...'

'Oh, anything. I don't mean rocks or a floating piece of timber, because they can sink any boat. But perhaps a wave even, if it hit awkwardly. One never knows. It might be good for ten years and it might go tomorrow. Like the rotten pear, squish.'

'Did he know?' asked Natalie. 'I mean before you saw?'

'Not at all. He had a bad shock; the tears stood in his eyes. And I was sorry for him, because that boat means everything to him. Good boat, too.' He went on with the net, thoughtfully; looked up suddenly. 'He asked you for money and you didn't give it him because you thought it was a trick?'

'Yes,' soberly. 'I made a mistake.'

'Well,' shrugging, lighting a cigarette. 'It is not a tragedy. He has doubtless gone away in a big emotion. But as you have seen, he always comes back.' He grinned. 'He makes a drama – it is for him very serious. Pardi, so much the worse for him.' He changed the subject abruptly. 'The barometer has fallen heavily, and the sky says we are going to have a hard mistral. Wherever he is, he'd better stay there now.'

'Where d'you think he could be?'

'He might be at Giens for diesel oil. We can find out – look at that boat there, he has been over. Hey, Agostino,' he

bellowed, 'seen *Olivia* in Giens?' A young fisherman, saunter-
ing along the jetty.

'Eh, Christophe. Bonjour, Madame,' politely. 'No, but, he
was there yesterday. Cleared out this morning without waiting for oil. Went out early, but perhaps he saw the barometer.
There is going to be a mistral.' He sauntered on.

'Perhaps he is out by the Langoustier, if he had a net down
last night.'

'Christophe,' she said, 'could we go out and look?'

'With pleasure. As long as we do not stay out too long. If
there is going to be a bad mistral, you do not want to be
caught. Neither does he,' reflectively. 'But I think it will be an
hour or two before it is anything.'

'I would like to very much. You see, I would like to . . .'

'All right. If you don't mind steering, I will finish my net.'

He pushed the boat out with an oar, and stooped to the
motor. Rumble, rumble, it went, and they were moving with
sudden surprising speed. He said nothing, but sat on the hatch
busy with his net. The water was still quite calm; out in the bay
Natalie gazed with interest at the castle of the Saracens, that
she had never seen from seaward.

Raymond was looking at the sky too. A look of mistral
about that, he thought. He had forgotten to look at the barometer since getting out here; hm, it had tumbled sharply in the
night.

He had been tucked away in an obscure bay behind the little
rocky island called the Langoustier since dawn. He had reckoned on this being a good alibi. He had slipped very quietly
out of the harbour of Giens without using the motor, before
anyone was stirring; he had not been seen. There was nothing
to say that he had not left the night before. He was very tired;
it was time to get back to harbour before the wind began and
the sea got up; he had overslept. Hm, he didn't suppose he
would see Natalie any more. She would surely be gone, now . . .

It had been easy; everything had been easy. Little minor
local difficulties, but in principle . . . easy. They had run a few
risks, and he had – agreed – done one thing that was very
stupid. Still, they had made a very fair haul. The Corse would

be quietly back in Cannes. He was here. There was nothing – absolutely nothing – to point to either of them having been anywhere near Saint-Tropez last night.

'I'll stand close up to the wall and you get on my shoulders.'

'I'm up.'

'It's only fifteen feet. Throw me the end of your belt ... All right, I've got a foothold now.' The Corsican was lying on the outhouse roof; Raymond breathed heavily and scrabbled with his feet, Jo's belt cutting into his fingers.

'Quiet.' Once the action started, it was the Corse who took charge. He was the active one, the athlete. Raymond felt the familiar old slowness and clumsy awkwardness; he scraped his forearms badly on the edge of the wall. But they were up, perched on the outhouse roof. No longer visible from the street, but very visible from the house, should any old woman chance to look out of the window. There was a sort of tiny courtyard. From where they were it was fairly easy to reach a mansard window by way of the wall, a drainpipe and the tiles. That is to say, for the Corsican it was fairly easy; for Raymond it was not easy at all, but he thought of climbing a mast, determined that he could do it, and did it.

The wooden shutters outside the window were closed, but only with a hook; the Corse, lying on his belly, opened them by slipping his knife-blade through the crack. The window was less easy. The old-fashioned type, locked by a vertical bolt in the middle which is closed by a half-turn on the window-catch; they are solid as rock. For five agonized minutes they worked on it with scotch tape and a glass-cutter; at last Jo got an arm through and turned the bolt. It all made noise, but not a big noise, except to them. A sort of scrattling noise, as though rats had got into the attic.

The attic was full of dust, mould, and close-shut stuffiness. It attacked the membranes of Raymond's nose, naughtily. He would strangle if he did not sneeze, but he would not sneeze. Sneeze he did, with a shatter. It seemed to discharge the tension in him. Craven fear and physical pain had mounted in him dangerously. Breathlessness, the throat-aching aftermath of effort, the struggle to hold it in and the exquisite pleasure of letting it explode. Fear and excitement and greed: it all flew together with spit, over a decrepit pram mostly. The Corse glared furiously; Raymond wanted to laugh. He felt so much better now.

'That'll bring the old one out for sure.'

'So much the better. I didn't want to go in her room.' They were struggling with their false noses. How to explain? – that he could not, not to save his life, have crept into some stuffy over-furnished little room, where an old woman lay snoring in a smell of mice and perished lavender, cheap soap and petit-beurre biscuits, probably with her teeth in a cracked glass and a pot in the middle of the floor. It was this kind of idea that made petty crime difficult for Raymond. The Corse did not have these scruples.

The door creaked abominably; on the other side of the landing, facing the street in front, was the larger attic, where the railwayman lived. The brown lino was worn away by thirty years of feet, but strangely it was polished and shining. It was the kind of detail that always struck Raymond, who always polished his own lino with such scrupulous self-respect.

Another door creaked, on the landing below.

'That you, Monsieur Manni?' came an extraordinary growling voice, hoarse from sleep. 'At this time – how is it possible?' When there was no answer she started to climb the steep stairs, puffing.

'What's the matter – you sick? ... But answer, then. Why haven't you put the light on?' Light came out of her doorway below. There was no light on the stairs – probably she had taken the bulb out for the sake of economy. For this kind of old woman a 'minuterie' time switch is too expensive.

She cleared her throat with a loud hawk and puffed.

'Hey, what's going on here? You drunk, or what?' She seemed to be wearing some extraordinary garment as a dressing-gown. So far as he could judge, it had once been a Persian lamb coat, dating from about nineteen thirty-six, absurdly straight and long.

'What the hell you playing at, Manni?' The rough words made Raymond feel better, but did not give him the courage to grab her. This was the part he had dreaded.

The Corse did not hesitate. Old women were fair game. Except his granny. She was a classical Fate, Moses and God the Father. Always had been, always would be. But other – all other – old women were his natural enemies; had been since he was five, and had stolen fruit and cheap sweeties and empty bottles (to get money back on them later) from the dark, astonishingly untidy little shops of other old women exactly like this. One, unexpectedly swift on her ancient feet, had chased him and landed him a frightful crack with a carpet-beater. He was going to pay that back, a bit. He flew out of the railwayman's opened door, like one of the big lizards that sit sunning themselves on the rocks of Porquerolles, and can move with such amazing speed.

'Awk,' she went; there was a thump and the Corse had bundled the coat over her head.

'String, string, string. Quick Ramon,' in a hiss. He looked like a tiny boy that has been told to carry a large goose to market.

'Awk,' again in the second before the Corse slapped a huge piece of sticking-plaster across her ancient, rather bearded chops. Raymond, in torchlight, observed four plastic haircurlers. One was bright blue, one yellow, and two were poison-green.

'Can she breathe?'

'Sure. Not come to her last glass of white wine yet, have you, my old? Nice and comfy, there. Now you lie quiet and go nicely to sleep, I'll cover you with a rug.'

There seemed to be an awful lot of stairs down. It wasn't as far as this going up the outside wall, thought Raymond, ludicrously. Carefully, they shut the old woman's door after turning the light out. A cheap old alarm clock was ticking lunatically away and the Corse launched a tremendous kick at the cat, which dodged adroitly and shot up the stairs.

A narrow passage that had last been whitewashed in Monsieur Clémenceau's day led to the street door. At one side was the door into the shop, that had perhaps been left as a fire-insurance condition. There were two bolts though, as well as the spring lock. They had to be sawed through; it took a very long time and was horribly hard work. Raymond did one, rather pleased because he managed it quicker than the Corse did. The street door was only two feet away, a solid affair enough but with a peculiar gap on one side that let through a piercing draught and a thin vertical needle of light. It was unpleasant to work cramped and sweating, and at the same time exposed to the sharp edge of cold draught, and Raymond had an uneasy feeling that they could well be in full view of a stray passer-by. Once they stopped and stayed very still as two policemen passed on foot, wheeling their bicycles.

'So there were a hundred thousand tons of apricots more than usual,' said a furry voice a yard away. 'They still ought to have paid an agreed minimum price to protect the growers.'

'Yeh,' answered a deeper, burry voice. 'They'll do that, same time they give us our pension rise.'

Boots faded grittily along the street and Raymond dripped more oil on the bolt, sweating as though in a Turkish bath. What filthy things rubber gloves were. His false nose stood carefully on the floor beside him, grinning insanely upwards. It was impossible to say which was the more disagreeable job, to stretch upwards to the top bolt, or to cramp downwards to the bottom.

The Corse put the cold chisel in the crack and the spring lock gave way; tearing out of the wood with a long grating sigh. They were in.

The shop was ordinary enough: just a picture-shop like any other, cluttered with pictures and frames. The display window was masked by aluminium venetian blinds. There was a good smell, of wood and canvas, of linseed and acetone and varnish, with faint taints of perfume – or was it just fly-spray? – of the thick rubber tiles underfoot, of a vase of flowers in the corner that needed changing. The perfume – no, it must be fly-spray, Raymond decided – was synthetic freesia, rather horrible.

At the back, a little double free-arch staircase had been built, with a delicate wrought-iron balustrade that curved upwards to each corner of a shallow little balcony. The good business was done up here. The first floor had been taken over too, thought Raymond, leaving the old woman her room, and the tiny kitchen and landing.

'Up.' Yes, there was a tiny gallery, a picture on an easel, two red-velvet chairs for the red-velvet customers. Behind was a cubby-hole of an office, where the woman who ran Fred Servaz's business for him could hang her coat and wash her hands and do the accounts and make coffee with an electric percolator. There was a little steel office desk, and a narrow filing cabinet. Both were broken easily with the cold chisel. Neither held any money.

Correspondence, book-keeping, catalogues. A bank passbook in a plastic cover, a tin of vacuum-pack coffee, a pair of white gloves needing washing, a Limoges powder-compact, and a tin of talcum-powder – they used this, gratefully, on their hands; the rubber gloves were vile. They discovered scratch-pads full of mysterious memos, phone-books, a half-full bottle of cognac, which cheered them up, a packet of Tampax, three ballpoint pens, and the paper and carbons for a portable typewriter. Not a penny or a smell of one.

The Corsican threw his glass furiously at a naked woman with disagreeable contours.

'Quiet,' said Raymond sharply. He was in command again now that they were in; it was strange how the authority changed hands wordlessly, 'Are those curtains safe?' The torch shot gleams everywhere; he switched on the desk lamp and sat down to study the pass-book. No, quite definitely, nothing had been paid in for eleven days.

'Can he have taken it already?'

'But he wasn't going back till Monday. He said he was staying in Porquerolles as long as he could.'

'Must be here somewhere. Wall safe? Behind one of the pictures maybe? We're buggered then.'

'Hardly. She was accustomed to bank every evening. I think she's dreamed up some hiding place, some real woman's trick. We've got to be patient.' He turned a Chinese vase upside down and shook it. Stepping backwards he knocked the easel down with a tremendous crash. They both stood shaking but paralysed for several minutes, gazing at a pen drawing of the Esterel range. At last the silence reassured them both.

'Try below again.'

Here it was difficult; they dared not risk the torch because of the venetian blinds, through which a little light would invariably percolate. They groped in dimness among artists' materials; brushes and stretchers and racks of paint-tubes. Nothing.

It was Raymond who found it. Right by the street door, a massive affair of chrome steel and double armour glass. Here, he was in full view of the street, and there was more light. He felt horribly exposed, but had a look around just the same. Pushing aside a split-cane screen he found a cupboard of painted plywood, tall, narrow, shallow. Electricity meters, no doubt. So it proved, after he had broken his knife-blade getting it open. But on top of the meters – there it was. The leather wallet that banks use for night-safes – and pleasantly full too, its stomach bulging like the soapstone Buddha there behind the counter. Behind was a manila envelope – the float for the till, evidently. Mostly small change – never mind, it will just pay our expenses. We do not despise small change.

They went back upstairs to the office, and turned on the table lamp to gloat. The little bag was locked, but after a struggle they got a knife through the stiff leather, tearing the contents slightly in doing so. Never mind; notes are often torn. And as for the cheques, who cared? No good to them. There were several cheques, and some of those accursed American Express things. But there was a fair amount of real money – portraits of Napoleon. Negotiable. Nice.

Enough to have made it worth while. When they split it in exact halves, laboriously, it all came to seven thousand one hundred and three francs each.

They could just as easily have done this later, outside. Honour, however, dictated that it should be done on the spot, instantly. It took too long. From downstairs there came in the silence a faint jingle. Something – a bunch of keys – had clattered slightly against the glass door.

Fred knew, of course, where Delphine left money on the rare occasions when it was not banked immediately. He did not bother to turn on lights – in fact he knew where money was, but not where switches were. There was plenty of light from the street. Hey – the little cupboard was open, just when he had taken a good minute fumbling for the little key on the ring, too. Delphine must have lost hers. It was of no importance. He did not at first notice that the cupboard had been forced but when he did he was not fussed. One loses keys, and the electricity man comes to read the meter, so one forces a little sixpenny lock with a knife-blade. But because it had been forced, Delphine – women's logic, that – had concluded that the cupboard was no longer a safe hiding-place. Mm, she would have left the bank-bag in the desk, doubtless, knowing he was coming to pick it up. Holding his bunch of keys, his finger on the little brass key to the wallet, he clumped up the staircase in the dark.

The two heroes were standing by the desk with their mouths open. They had not counted on this. An old woman – familiar, planned against, provided for – was one thing: a man, possibly alert and strong, possibly even armed – was another. Still, the Corsican was not one to go on standing like a frozen rabbit. Directly his senses told him there was one man only, and that man careless, unsuspecting, half asleep – he could hear Fred distinctly below, fidgeting with his keys and muttering – he unwound. He moved gently behind the curtain that shut the little office off, admirably placed to pull a man's jacket over his arms from behind. The false nose peered behind the curtain, ludicrously.

Raymond was frightened though, badly frightened. He knew that it was Fred. He hadn't thought of this, hadn't planned against it. He stood rigid with terror. On the balcony, Fred turned the lights on.

Raymond stared at the Corse as though appealing for help. The false nose projecting from the red-velvet curtain looked like Cyrano de Bergerac – what did that remind him of? Did it remind him of Pauline? And of another occasion when he had stood with his mouth open being calmly knocked to pieces by another casual, rich, confident gentleman? It was not, certainly, Fred he attacked. Was it the writer of cheques – Mr Artur de Beaugency?

Instead of staying still and waiting for the Corse to make a quiet neat job, he suddenly rushed across the room, not even aware that he had picked up the cold chisel.

Fred was concerned with absolutely nothing at that moment

except a long boring drive to Paris. He was thinking vaguely of a sandwich somewhere, and balancing the advantages of a big bowl of coffee – steaming in curls, wonderful-smelling – against those of a bottle of pilsener – misty, cool, beckoning, beautifully sharp and fresh to a mouth that has smoked too much. He was utterly flabbergasted at the sudden sight of a false nose hurtling at him. He stood stupidly with his hand still out towards the light switch, wondering ludicrously why it should be carnival time. There was some local feast in April, when the Tropéziens fired off cannons and made a great hullabaloo generally. He had just about got as far as wondering what day it was when the cold chisel took him just above the ear and he stopped caring.

'That's settled him,' said Raymond.

'You're a fool, all the same,' said the Corse, calmly. 'He might have yelled, or hit you first.'

'Let's get out of here.'

'What you want to clonk him for – there was plenty of string left. And that steel thing – why not just punch him in the guts? An inch or so farther forward and you could just as easily have killed him, bird-brain.'

'We've got what we want. Let's jump.'

'And have the first flatfoot that sees the door open find him? Take the keys and lock the door, you clunk. No great harm done – except to his head, perhaps. If we lock up it's odds who finds who first, the railway fellow, or the woman here when she opens the shop. Neither'll be here before eight.'

'I'll just see if he's all right.'

'I'll lock the doors, then.' The Corsican's admiration for Raymond's head had gone down a good deal. But one does not abandon one's friends in a crisis. That is the unforgivable crime. Waiting quietly by the door back to the passage, the Corse was thinking that Raymond, after all, had planned the job, and found the money. Alone, the Corse could have knocked people on the head – but he could not have climbed the wall. It was Raymond that had thought of the glass-cutter and the scotch tape, the sticking-plaster and the electricity meter. As well as discovering that there was money here after

126

all. The seven thousand francs restored Raymond's shaken credit.

Raymond put a red-velvet cushion under Fred's head. He had nothing against Fred, and hoped he was not badly injured. He hadn't been hit that hard, and the blow had half glanced. It was not like – well, like a gun. Still, it was robbery with violence now. They'd better not get caught. He was breathing fairly normally; Raymond felt his pulse. It was there anyway. Oh come, he wasn't dead.

A quarter of an hour later they were on the scooter on the way back to Le Lavandou. And in another half-hour they would be in the car. It was all arranged. They had dumped the string, the noses, the plaster, the slit bank-bag, the cheques. Once in Giens, Raymond would push straight off with the boat. The Corse would drive direct back to Cannes through Fréjus.

There, he had planned, he would pick up the lily of the valley and head off to Italy. He had still said nothing about this idea to Raymond. Seven thousand – that would make a nice holiday. That would certainly mean a honeymoon in Portofino. The little English coupé flew back through the Maures like a tomahawk.

Chapter Thirteen

Raymond, on his way back to harbour, met Christophe's boat, with Natalie in it, just off the point, He was, at first, frightened. Both boats rocked to the motion of the other and to that of the sea, which was beginning to get up, though there was, as yet, hardly any wind. The two motors thudded nervously in neutral, only three or four metres apart.

'Hey, Christophe.'

'Bonjour, Capitaine.'

'There's going to be a big mistral. I've been out by the Langoustier all night.'

'Catch anything?'

'Not worth speaking of.'

Natalie had been staring at the point, at the 'castle', as though tactfully. Now she turned towards him suddenly.

'May I board you?' He was much flustered. But what could he say, with Christophe there too – grinning, the stinker, amused by Raymond's embarrassment.

'If you want to – of course.' Christophe brought the boat delicately alongside, watching it carefully.

'You'll have to jump, Madame. You can – don't be alarmed.'

'I'm not in the least alarmed.' She jumped neatly. Christophe turned his boat, the arc swinging away from them, and picked up speed. The fishing boat, lighter and smaller than *Olivia*, and with finer lines, was faster through the water. So so, Christophe was thinking, cheerfully: they all lived happily ever after. Women are a comedy.

Natalie was embarrassed too, certainly. She knew what to say, but was not very happy with her dialogue, so she said nothing. Oh, a few banalities.

'Going to be a mistral, I hear.'

'Yes, a bad one by the look of it. We've got to get back to

128

harbour.' He had put the motor full ahead, and was steering in Christophe's wake. 'The sea will get up nastily – short and sudden.'

'No fish, then?'

'I threw back what there was – not even enough to make a bouillabaisse. You haven't been out there, by the Langoustier?'

'I don't think so.' Silence, till he slowed to pick up the mooring, and made himself unnecessarily busy knotting the warp.

'I wasn't at all polite,' she said suddenly, 'when I saw you last. I wanted to apologize.' She did not try to explain what she was doing on Christophe's boat. 'I thought – I don't know what I thought. I acted on impulse, as I too often do. I regretted it. Maybe I'll regret this too.'

Raymond did not know what to say.

'I thought you were concocting a hard-luck tale,' she went on; her voice was uninflected, monotonous. 'I was mad at you, and madder at myself. It hurt me to think you should try a cheap gag on me – just to see if I would undo my purse as well as my trousers. I have a lot of vanity.'

Raymond's mouth was full of teeth, but he had to say something. 'Come down to the cabin.' The mistral was beginning to blow, all right. The boat was starting to rock slightly at the mooring. 'Would you like a drink?' He still had half a bottle of the whisky left by the Corse. Damn it, for him things were always simple. Why do they always have to be so damn complicated for me, then?

'Yes.' She watched him pour, took the glass, drank half quickly. 'I have come to the conclusion that I behaved in a small-minded, mean way. I realize that you could do nothing with the boat unmended. That you needed that money.'

'Yes, I did, I mean I do.' He drank whisky himself, too fast. He had seven thousand francs, hidden in rather a good place too. Better than a meter cupboard. He had been thinking, during what was left of the night, after he had got out to the Langoustier.

The money was not identifiable: there would be nothing to say it wasn't his. It was enough to mend *Olivia*'s hull three times over. Or it would be enough to live on for a year, comfortably, added to his income. But not in Porquerolles. Christophe would wonder. Everybody would wonder. He had been thinking of going back to Portugal. He could get the boat mended there well and cheaply. And now Natalie was offering him money. The same money.

Everything was suddenly different. He felt humiliated. Whatever he did, he always felt humiliated, didn't he? But he did not think that he had ever felt quite so humiliated as at this moment.

'How much would it cost?' she asked suddenly. 'One thousand? Two?'

Words stumbled out of him.

'Two would certainly do it, I think.'

'It's my own money, in my account. Nothing to do with my husband, if that's what's bothering you.' She looked at his face. Anybody would think she had hit him. She should have kept her mouth shut, maybe. It might have been better to have written a cheque, put it in his hand, and gone immediately away. She was stuck with this scene now. It was a bad scene; she should have known better than to try to play it.

'Are you furious that Christophe told me about the boat? I asked him. He knew nothing about it. About the money, I mean.'

'Yes. I mean no. I mean I know.' A slightly harder gust of wind; a halyard slapped against the mast.

'If you're ashore this evening I'll give you a cheque. For five thousand. For the repairs, and any left over is to pay for my being a bastard. Stores, or anything you need. You'll need money, won't you, wherever you pause, or land for water, or whatever it is you do.' God, she thought, what nonsense I'm talking. Why on earth have I made this scene?

The whole thing seemed like ... like ... totally unreal anyway, thought Raymond. Too much like a bad joke. Anybody would think that she knew her husband had been robbed. And knew I had done it.

'You're staring,' she said, 'exactly as though I had hit you over the head. What's the matter? I know I'm behaving very stupidly myself, but this is not important. It's only money. It was just my stupidity that made it important.'

It was almost too good to be true, he thought. He wished he

felt capable of speaking. And normally I'm fluent enough, he told himself. But just at these moments when I could wish to find something adequate to say, I stand there planted. He was reminded again of the little 'conference room' in the Hôtel des Indes, and Monsieur de B. in his well-cut horseman's trousers and his misty grey-green tweed jacket. A nice colour; he recalled it very well; Natalie had a pair of linen slacks the same colour. A sage green, one could call it.

'You'd better bring me ashore, if you will,' said Natalie. 'I've made a mess of what I came to say. And the whole village will be concluding that we're making love here. Not that I care, particularly. I won't be staying much longer. I simply want you to do one thing. To go. To get the boat mended and go. Will you do that?'

'Yes.' How long was this going to go on? He had to get away from here, mistral or no mistral.

They both started suddenly at a loud bump. A strong open hand had hit the hull, outside. Christophe's voice called loudly. 'Holà. Holà, there.'

Raymond was glad of the interruption. He climbed the companion. 'What's the matter with you?'

'Madame Servaz still there? Can I come up?'

That Christophe, thought Natalie with a moment at last of humour and detachment. Always tactful. Did he really think, then, that they were making love?

'Sure you can come up.'

Christophe looped the dinghy painter carelessly round a cleat, jumped up deftly and slid down the companion.

'Ah, Madame. I've been at the hotel; I was going home with my fish. They've just had a telephone message. When I said I knew where you were they asked me to bring it.'

One of Fred's dramas, no doubt, thought Natalie. He'd be in Paris, she supposed, by this time. She felt an impatient indifference. She was bored by the idea of Fred. Let him enjoy himself in auction rooms, and not bother her for a few days, hm?

Still, it was an opportune arrival. This scene had gone off in a way that she didn't understand, and had disconcerted her. She would go ashore with Christophe, and be rid of embarrassment.

Raymond knew what was coming. It would have to happen here. Here on his boat, in the centre of his life. He couldn't stop it, however badly he wanted to get away.

'I don't want to frighten you, but the message is that your husband had some sort of accident. But he's not dead or anything.'

There was silence for a moment while Natalie gathered all her powers of self-control.

'Driving too fast, I suppose,' in a calm voice. 'Is he badly hurt?' Forgive me, Fred, she was thinking.

'Fairly badly, they said, but not dangerously. He's in hospital being cared for – in Saint-Tropez.'

'I must go at once. I suppose Michel can take me.'

Raymond had got his tongue back now that Natalie had forgotten his very existence.

'I can take you if you like. It goes slower, of course, but by the time you'd got ashore and found Michel I could have brought you.'

'There's that. Would you, Raymond? Isn't it too much trouble?'

That's the first time she has ever used my name, he thought. And she spoke with tenderness, because now she is able to set me outside her thoughts finally.

'I have to go to Giens anyway for oil. The mistral's not bad enough yet to stop me.'

'My car's in Toulon, too,' she said absently, not even listening. 'I'll just have to take a taxi, that's all.'

'I can tell them you've gone, then?' said Christophe, sliding into the dinghy. 'You aren't going ashore for anything?'

'No. But Christophe –' she was holding out a fifty franc note. 'Will you give that to the chambermaid and ask her to pack and put my things on the boat? I'll ring up from there. They'll understand.'

'But of course, Madame.'

Raymond was busy starting the motor. 'Slip the mooring for me, Christophe, will you?'

Christophe untied the warp and threw it on board. The dinghy drifted away directly he let go. He gave an abrupt wave and began to row. Raymond returned it; *Olivia* was already gathering way, biting into the rising sea with a short pitching motion. It would take them nearly half an hour to cross the Petite Passe. The wind was making a thin keening noise now in the rigging.

Natalie spoke her thoughts.

'Three days ago I was in love with you. Two days ago I thought you were a mean, cheap little crook.'

'I wish you'd stayed thinking so.'

'Now – I'll send you a cheque. As one does to pay a dentist's bill. I would never have believed it possible.'

Porquerolles was fading behind them to an indistinct mass of tree-clad rock. The jetty was still visible, and the spot of red marking the tiny tower. On the highest point of the island, the 'semaphore', as the weather station with its radar beacons was still called, showed like a tooth above the trees. It is like a tiny white castle out of a fairy-tale, she thought. It is classical to believe in fairy-tales on islands, but I have got too deeply involved in one. It is a good thing that I should now return to the mainland, to a world of reality, of writing cheques and auto accidents and taxis. It was time.

This boy – I found him in a fairy-tale. I spoilt it by trying to join in. It is necessary for me to return at once to reality. But he must stay. She turned again to watch the mainland creeping closer.

I have to tell her, thought Raymond. It's no use: I have to tell her. I suggested bringing her because I knew I would have to face this last opportunity of telling her.

'Don't forget your promise,' she said. 'Remember that it is very important for me as well as for you.'

'It's too late,' shouted Raymond suddenly.

'What do you mean, too late?'

'Because you will tell the police.' They were both swaying to keep balanced in the pitching boat. 'Your husband hasn't had any auto accident. I hit him.'

'But why did you hit him?' softly, reasonably. It did not make much sense. 'He had done you no harm.'

'He interrupted me robbing his shop,' very loudly. 'He came

133

in suddenly – it was dark – I was startled – I was where I couldn't run, or anything – I hit him. Quite unnecessarily,' he added in a more normal tone.

There. He had done, at last, something he need not feel ashamed of. Not confessing. More that for once he had spoken out. He hadn't lost his tongue, hadn't just kept a shamefaced silence.

'Oh ... my poor boy.'

The tone brought him back to his accustomed feeling of deflation. She simply sounded a little sorry for him.

'You robbed the shop ... I see. Because you heard him say that he had saved up money there ... I see ... But really because I insulted you more than because I had refused to give you money ... Still, you needed that money. So you took it ... And now I have turned the knife by behaving like a perfect fool, and offering you the money after all. Another insult ... Did you get any money? Or did even that go wrong?'

'No,' dully. 'I got the money.'

'How much?' in the tone of a woman asking the price of a pair of stockings. It bewildered him. Hadn't she understood?

'But I tell you it was me who hit your husband. If he's in hospital it was me who put him there. I cracked his head with a cold chisel.'

Out of the fairy-tale and into reality. There was an Irish play about a young man who boasts that he did the same thing. 'I felled my dad with a stroke of loy,' he boasts. What was a loy? wondered Natalie.

'Don't shout. I heard you the first time. I said how much?'

He felt helpless, drowned in incomprehension and impotence.

'Seven thousand. That was only half, though.'

'Half? Oh, I see: you had a helper. Or was it him who hit Fred?' She might have been discussing the weather.

He made a last effort to pierce the veil.

'You must go to the police. I'll tell them everything.'

'What have the police to do with this?'

'I've committed a crime.'

Silence again. They were not more than five minutes off the little landing stage on the Giens peninsula.

134

'I see,' she said. 'You want to go and tell the police. That will make you feel a bit of a hero, no doubt. Nice for the police to know about our little affair. Nice for Fred, to learn that my caprices put him in hospital with a cracked skull. He would no doubt get a big laugh from my telling him "It was a lover of mine, darling, who hit you, but don't worry, here's the money back".' Her voice was dry and level. 'The insurance will pay this money. Now shut up. I don't wish to hear any more about this. Just keep that great yap of yours closed from now on, to the police and everybody else. You could just as easily have kept quiet – then you'd have had twelve thousand. As it is, regard whatever you've got as a present from me, or as a pay-off cheque – whichever you prefer. And don't worry. You're not a cheap crook, as I thought. You're simply a rather pathetic person. And now silence.'

The boat slowed; Raymond reversed the screw and put the rudder over. Natalie was standing by the bulwark, holding on to a shroud; for an instant, the attitude reminded him of the day in Port-Cros.

The boat touched gently against the wooden piles; she jumped ashore, and turned with a face of conventional politeness.

'Thank you very much indeed for bringing me across; that was very kind.' Her back was to him already, scanning the row of cars. 'Taxi. Toulon, please, and drive as fast as you like.'

Raymond put the motor into reverse. He had to go around the little point, to the fishing harbour, to get diesel oil.

Chapter Fourteen

Jo the Corse had with typical confidence not waited for the result of the raid to make his plans. When he had spoken to Dominique on the phone, and understood what Raymond had in mind, he had packed a case with the things he had on the yacht, and carted it into Cannes. If this came off, he would lose no time, and run no risk, in going back to the yacht. And after dropping Raymond in Giens he had driven back along the corniche of the Maures in high good humour.

Seven thousand francs: not a bad night's work. Raymond was not perhaps totally reliable in action, but he was a good planner. The Corse did not feel entirely happy about Fred lying there on the floor – but going over things in his mind he was confident that nothing could give them away. Even the tennis shoes had been ditched. There was no risk in his leaving Cannes. How many others left the same day, without knowing or caring that a robbery had been committed in Saint-Tropez?

If everything was so free from risk, why had he not told Raymond? Had he been just a bit worried lest Raymond disapprove, or produce a good contrary argument? Why was he feeling a scrap guilty at having kept his plan secret?

The hell with it. It was perfectly safe, and none of Raymond's business, anyway. There was nothing further of any value to be got from Vin – it was on all counts time to change horizons, to find new pastures to graze upon.

In Cannes he picked up his lily. She loved him hugely, and it was very understandable. To her he was a soldier of fortune. Beau Geste. If the Corse had known about Beau Geste he would have been greatly impressed. These English aristocrats with their quaint codes of honour – practically Corsican, that was. He would have understood them very well.

*

Mr Vincent Proctor was not happy. Now Jo had been told often enough that this trailing of slummy little sluts around bars was inadmissible. Grave loss of face for him, Vincent – anyway an undignified, even squalid performance. Mr Proctor's Swedish engineer – who copied his master's technique in a small way – was a great haunter of bars. He had seen the English lily, and had been greatly shocked. He had felt it his duty to tell Mr Proctor all about it; he had found Patricia squalid, definitely, in the highest degree.

It was a breach of confidence, thought Mr Proctor, and good faith. If Jo continued to disregard one's plain wishes and the code of behaviour, it was from vice. One had often feared there was a vicious streak in that boy. Undeniably, it added powerfully to his attractions. Still, this had now gone far enough. One would now be forced, distasteful though it was, to say something indelicate. No time like the present, either.

It occurred to Mr Proctor that Jo would probably not be back before evening, and that this might be a good opportunity to have a thorough look around the boy's cabin. If one found indiscretions, those would be pieces of conviction, as the French put it.

Mr Proctor blew a plume of smoke, put down his drink, got out of his deckchair lightly – aha, one was still slim and youthful, thanks to Yoga – and strolled delicately across the afterdeck.

'Have you seen Jo, Maurice?' It was just a precaution.

'Why, yes sir. 'Bout an hour ago he was here, but he left again. Had a suitcase. Wasn't he going to the Casino tonight with you?'

'It wasn't quite decided on.' Indeed, Master Jo.

He padded along the companionway and found he did not need his master key. Jo's key dangled in the lock.

Hm, and more hm, and a nasty little pulse that throbbed unpleasantly in one's temple, and certainly meant a disagreeable time ahead for everyone on the yacht. One would have to drink nothing but Evian for a week – one's blood pressure. The cabin had been cleaned out. All the clothes one had given Jo – not that one had ever made him look civilized, but one enjoyed that decorative barbaric look. Ties, shoes, a very good pair of cuff-links. A crystal lighter – one did a rapid sum in one's mind, and was slightly put out to notice the figure arrived at by several rather pretty little presents. Suddenly, Mr Proctor was very angry indeed. Jo had cleared out.

And the car? That had not been a present – well – no, definitely, not a present. One remembered one's own words quite clearly.

'Here is the key to a little auto, my dear. Regard it as yours as long as you are with us. I trust it will amuse you.'

'Maurice, I am going ashore. If I should not be back by six-thirty, serve the apéritif on the afterdeck. I will certainly be back for dinner.'

'Very good, sir.'

Twenty minutes later, upright and youthful, Mr Proctor walked springily on expensive black and white buckskin shoes into the Cannes police bureau.

'I wish to see the Commissaire; here is my card. Be kind enough to tell him that I am waiting. I would have rung first, but I am pressed. You may say that it is urgent, and may lead to the laying of a criminal charge.'

The Commissaire chewed his spectacles and looked at the card without enthusiasm.

'Isn't this the old queen off the big white vedette in the harbour?'

'That's him, patron.'

'Oh, very well; I'll see him.'

'It is a scandalous abuse,' one was saying five minutes later, not greatly impressed by the efficiency of this person. 'I wish to lay formal complaint, and shall ask the United States Consul to complain in Paris and to the Prefect if prompt action is not taken.'

The Commissaire laid down his glasses and lit a cigarette.

'I must point out, Mr Proctor, that you have shown me no evidence yet that the boy has stolen anything. These were all presents – mm? – and the auto too was a virtual gift.'

'Certainly not. Temporary use.'

138

'In whose name are the auto papers?'

'Mine, naturally.'

'Very well. But temporary use could perfectly reasonably mean a trip to Paris. An auto doesn't stay in one place, hm? It gets up and walks. At what point could it be established that this boy intends to steal your property? After what time lapse? He might be back this evening.'

'He has taken all his belongings. That indicates quite clearly that he does not intend to return.'

'Very well,' said the Commissaire, who was rather enjoying being tiresome. 'We still have no clear legal basis to lay a charge of theft. You gave him the auto keys. You told him to regard the auto as his up to a certain point, verbally expressed and extremely vague. I can see no basis for an arrest. The only demarcation line I could suggest would be a geographical one. If he attempts to pass the French frontier, that might stretch the construction he can put upon your words further than he could justify.'

'To pack and leave, without a word, is a clear indication of bad faith.'

'Possibly. One word, if you will allow. If you persist in giving boys expensive presents, you will certainly have further experiences of this nature. I am clear? Very well, Mr Proctor, we will do what we can. If the boy has merely gone for a fling round the countryside ... I will have a watch kept at frontiers. I must ask you to excuse me now.'

'Freedom, freedom, it's a wonderful thing,' said the Corsican, hurtling up and down the loops of the corniche. They had passed Nice, were near Eze. 'In another hour, we'll be in Menton, perhaps a nice drink, huh? And then, once over the border, ah, lovely Italy, with what pleasure I will show you. No more pests. That nosy Vincent, that endless snuffling. Every time I came back, throughout dinner a bloody catechism into everything I'd done. That is not for me. No yachts and no little cocktail canapés make up for freedom. Now – I have taken nothing but what I have been freely given, and good-bye United States, land of heroes. What I have put up with for imbecile tales of heroes. Those decorations on the breasts of pigeons. I have earned everything I have; that I can tell you. Wait till I show you Portofino. Ah, the joy of being alive.'

Patricia, very happy too, kissed the back of the hand that lay on the steering-wheel.

In Saint-Tropez, policemen were turning over what evidence there was to be found.

'Neat enough. Amateur, of course – what professional would go to such enormous trouble for so little? There was more than usual – they must have known that. And how! That'll be the key, no doubt. Very well, have everybody notified. All movements of traffic, frontiers of course, anyone who seems suddenly to have more money than they should. All unusual purchases or expenditures. The money always burns them; new suit straight off. Let's hope they're tempted to cash the cheques. All right, set it all going.'

'The wife's here, patron.'

'Show her in . . . My profound sympathies, Madame, I'm glad to say the doctor has already assured us that there's no permanent or grave damage. A few weeks rest . . . You've been to the hospital yourself, of course. We're doing what we can; excellent chance of clearing it up rapidly. Amateur gangsters, Madame,' with disdain.

'Now, just for the sake of form, is there anything you can tell us? I'm going on the assumption that they knew, some-how, that there was an unusual amount of money. Implies too great a coincidence, otherwise. Any notion at all, Madame, how that came to be known? Perhaps you might recall some word passed and overheard, a scrap of paper, a telephone call possibly? Some tiny indiscretion, no more than a slight lack of caution that would normally have no consequence?'

'None whatever, I'm afraid,' said Natalie calmly. 'I've no doubt you're right, though.'

'Why?'

'Why what?'

'Have you no doubt I'm right? The same thought occurred to you?'

140

'Not in those terms, but my husband is often incautious – he gets carried away by his enthusiasm. He didn't mention it in my presence that I recall.'

'But he mentioned it to you, of course.'

'Naturally – we spent the weekend together in Porquerolles.'

'Ah yes. We'll have to see what he can remember when he wakes up.'

Fred could remember very little when he woke up except that he had thought it was carnival time, which helped nobody much. He had a bad headache, but once reassured by a jovial surgeon that he wasn't going to die, he started taking an interest in life again. It would all be good publicity – the shop would do a roaring trade. It was something in return for those enormous insurance premiums. He was most indignant at the idea that he could possibly have been indiscreet. Not a soul could possibly have known, except Delphine, of course, and Natalie. He wanted a telephone, to ring his old lady in Saint-Cloud, but this was vetoed. Natalie must do it, then. He was reassured to hear the old biddy was sympathetic, even accommodating. That picture was his anyway, though it was undeniably a pity to miss the auction. Natalie booked a room at a hotel, rang Porquerolles to get her luggage forwarded, and rang Paris for some clothes that would be a bit less casual, and Fred's pyjamas. In this whirl of nurses and policemen she had plenty to keep her occupied. Once the headache was over, she foresaw, Fred would be a nuisance; she bought three or four paperback crime novels to keep him sweetened.

Raymond's oil- and water-tanks were full, but he walked up the hill to buy a few provisions. Not much; he didn't need much. Just enough for the first stage of a voyage. He had had enough of the Côte d'Azur, and enough of people too, for a long long while.

Where to? Canaries? Anyway, out of the Mediterranean, away from France. Why not the Canaries? It would be a good place to get the boat seen to, to have a refit. And if he could still not bear the sight of land – it was the first stage to Valparaiso.

141

Why not, after all? There was nothing stopping him – less than there ever had been.

There was a mistral blowing, of course, and looking like a bad one if it kept up. He was not frightened of it. He preferred it to the people one met, who all seemed to look at him with the same calm, unhostile expression, gave him a thousand pounds, as though it were three-ha'pence, and asked him to be so good as to go far away.

Very well, he would. He had no fear of the wind. He thought a little of *Olivia*'s rotted and metal-patched hull, and shrugged. Either it would go, or it wouldn't. But there was no reason to despair. The mistral is only a wind. It brings up a short, snapping, angry sea, but it is not a storm like an Atlantic storm from the north-east, that tears up everything in its path. *Olivia* could carry sail under this wind, and ride the steep short breakers. On a westerly course, such as he intended to take, she would get a famous shove away from the land. And that, above all, was what he wanted. *Olivia* would have a good chance of carrying her wind all the way to Minorca. There he could rest, and think about risks, and the course to shape. There, he would be already far from France.

He had two anchors holding his mooring in Porquerolles. He wasn't going back for them. An anchor in Porquerolles was no longer anything he wanted. He did not feel like hauling anything up by the roots. What he wanted to make was one clean cut, now. Straight through.

At the frontier, by Ventimiglia, the Corse was holding out his papers casually. The passport officer glanced at his passport, at him, and then walked towards a customs officer who was waving on the man and the car in front. The customs man glanced at his driving licence and carnet.

'Logbook, please.' He ran an eye over the car.

'You're the owner of this car?'

' 'S right.'

'But this isn't the name that's on your passport. Proctor – who's that?'

'He was the owner all right. We never bothered changing the name on the registration.'

'But it's your car, you claim?'

'I don't claim anything. 'S my car.'

'How do you explain then that Mr Proctor complains that you have stolen his auto?'

The Corse stared in astonishment for a moment, and then grinned.

'I see how it is. The old bastard's mad at me, so he thinks up a tale to try and drop me in the purée.'

'That doesn't concern me. What I see is that the auto's registered to him, he complains of its theft – and you're driving it over the border.'

'But he gave it me.'

'Gave – or lent?'

'Gave, damn it.'

'And have you any paper or other evidence to bear out this gift?'

'Well, no, but . . .'

'Out.'

Corsican blood changed to fire.

'Skin of a cow, I'll . . .'

'Out. In the hut there.'

A fat brigadier was writing at a desk. He looked at the Corse with disfavour in a lack-lustre eye.

'The auto from Cannes, Brig. The American one.'

'Ah.' He dropped his pen and surveyed the smouldering Corsican at leisure. He hitched an expression of severity into small cunning eyes. 'And what are you proposing to do in Italy?'

'Going with my fiancée to visit my family before getting married,' virtuously.

'Really . . . That's a sudden change, isn't it?'

'What's it got to do with you?'

'You've been living on a boat in Cannes, haven't you?'

'I've broken with all that.'

'Haven't broken with the pretty things that went with it, seemingly.'

The Corse was clever enough to see he was being needled, controlled himself, and spoke patiently.

'Look – can't you see? I'm not denying it, but I'm normal,

thanks. He got mad at me because I wanted to marry a girl, so out of spite he's trying to make trouble.'

'Yes, yes, but all that doesn't interest me. I'm acting on a complaint made to the commissariat of police in Cannes. You can make all the explanations there.'

'Now listen . . .'

'I'm busy. Take them inside,' he said, pointing with his pen. 'Get the auto off the road and make an inventory of the contents. This Proctor geezer may have missed more things.'

A police car brought the Corse and the lily back to Cannes, with their belongings. The little sports auto was left in Vintimille – let that Proctor bother about it. The customs officers had searched it thoroughly, just to be tiresome because the Corsican had given lip, made a thorough search of it, and made an inventory while they were waiting for the police to arrive. A young inspector of police received them. He knew Mr Proctor and did not care for him any more than his superior officer. None of this was serious. Still, he would run the rule over the Corse, just for form. One of the items on the inventory did not seem quite right.

'So you were going to Italy. How long were you proposing to stay there?'

'How do I know? A few weeks maybe. I have relations, friends.'

'Quite expensive though, a holiday in Italy. Especially with Mademoiselle here.'

'Not especially.'

'I see that in your passport your profession is given as barman. You're on holiday – with the season just beginning?'

'I can find work easily in Italy,' sulkily.

'But you haven't been working lately?'

'What's it to you?'

'Just that I understand how you've been supporting yourself – don't trouble to deny that you've been living on this American – but how do you go about financing a holiday? Were you thinking perhaps of selling the car?'

'No I wasn't.'

'Explain to me what you were thinking of, a little.'

'Get screwed.'

The inspector didn't change expression. So, he was thinking. Why does he hide the fact that he has a large sum of money?

'How much have you got? If you have enough for a few weeks in Italy, we might not be so suspicious that your intention was to sell the car. Mr Proctor's car,' meaningly. 'As you knew perfectly well, whatever you say.'

'You've looked in my wallet,' sulkily.

'But I'm not interested in your wallet, I'm interested in the rest.'

'What rest?'

'The customs officers report finding a packet of notes amounting to five thousand francs in the spare wheel. It seems rather a lot of money for you to have. Is it yours?'

'Of course it's mine.'

'Why hide it there?'

'I like to keep things safe.'

'So you admit putting it there.'

'I don't admit anything. Nothing to admit.'

'Did you or didn't you?'

'Find out.'

'But there are fingerprints on the envelope,' sweetly. He didn't know whether there were or not, but it is a classic remark.

'I've nothing to say.'

'Hm.' The inspector got up and walked out of the room.

'Look, chief. This old froggio's auto. We've got the auto back, and we've got the boy here, with a girl. What we going to do, keep him? We've nothing much on him, have we? Possible attempted theft, which we couldn't easily prove, and why should we go to the trouble, just to satisfy the spite of that Proctor?'

The chief inspector shrugged; he was completely uninterested. 'Might as well give him a shaking and turn him loose. We've got the auto back. Proctor won't try and push the theft now – stands to lose too much face. The girl can go – better ask the patron if he wants the boy held.'

The chief inspector had not even bothered to look up from

his papers. He had one eye screwed up to keep the smoke from his cigarette from getting in it.

'There's just one thing. Boy had five thousand in notes hidden in the auto. He didn't mention it and more or less tries to wriggle out of accounting for it. Seems rather a lot, and as though fishy. He can't have pinched that from Proctor, surely?'

'Five thousand francs?' slowly. The chief inspector put his cigarette in the ash-tray and leaned back. 'Hidden in the auto? Has it been searched?'

'By customs in Vintimille. Spare wheel.'

'Better give them a ring. Have it searched again – really searched. Make sure there's no more.'

The inspector looked puzzled.

'Why should there be more? He had about two thousand in his wallet.'

'Haven't you seen this?' holding up a strip of paper. 'Break in in Saint-Trop last night; came on the telex.'

'Hadn't got round to it yet. But I see what you mean.'

It was all rather a nice way out of it. They would phone Mr Proctor virtuously, telling him in honeyed words that his car was to be found at the frontier – and let him go and tow it back. The problem of whether to hold the Corse or not could be solved cleverly by shifting him off to Saint-Trop. Let them bother about it. Even if it had nothing to do with them, this Corse was clearly a cheeky lad – it wouldn't hurt anyone to keep him in storage a few hours. That way, they were rid of a nuisance.

Saint-Tropez was interested. They would like a little word with this Corsican. And about the time that Raymond was leaving Giens, while Natalie was driving over from Toulon, and while Fred was still semi-conscious in a hospital bed, a second police car went to ferry Jo and his loyal – still bewildered – lily over to Saint-Tropez. They arrived, together with the message that there was no more money to be found in the auto, just after Natalie had left to go to a hotel.

Chapter Fifteen

They started cheerfully enough; it looked quite promising. A boy with a dubious background, with no clear means of support and thus to police eyes riffraff, known too in the cafés of Saint-Tropez, had been picked up at the frontier the morning after a burglary, in a car that was not his, with five thousand francs he could not properly account for, on his way to Italy, to be quietly out of everyone's way. They rubbed their hands and prepared to carve him.

'Let's hear where you spent yesterday.'

'In Cannes.'

'Where else?'

'Nowhere else.'

'By yourself?'

'By myself.'

'Doing?'

'I had a sleep because I wanted to make an early start.'

'And you weren't near here at all, you claim?'

'Hadn't anything to do here.'

'You've friends here.'

'Who hasn't?'

The Corse, thoroughly wary and determined, wasn't going to give much away, and they had nothing but suppositions to go on. The old woman, unharmed it seemed by her night on the landing, was voluble but no great help, and Fred, who had been questioned directly he woke, could remember nothing. A tall boy in a carnival mask – well, nobody could call the Corse tall.

'You haven't anything on me, in Cannes or anywhere else, but you have a try at tying me to something that comes into your dim heads just because I've been here a couple of times.'

'Shut up. Now, we come to this money.'

'Some Proctor gave me. Some I won.'

'Five thousand?'

'Not all at once, of course. But over six months. He often gave money, and once or twice I've had good runs at the Casino and racing.'

'You're not seriously expecting us to believe that.'

'Look, he gave me an auto, which he's denying now out of spite, and a lot more things he can't deny.'

'So we'll ask him whether he ever gave you money.'

'He'll say no, of course,' contemptuously. 'You expect him to admit to being a bigger fool than he looks already? He's mad with me because I went off with a girl. They saw that straight off in Cannes. I couldn't prove he gave me the auto, but he can't prove he never gave me money.'

'But I'm still not satisfied with your story. You can wait till we check up on a few more things. Staying here won't do you any harm.'

It was quite true; the inspector was not satisfied. Having a thousand francs pressed affectionately into one's hand as though it were a couple of tens ... These rich pederasts were more careful with their money. Making a lucky win at the Casino ... And then carefully saving it all up – no. Not in character. It all had a fabricated sound; he didn't believe a word of it. He had the lily brought in alone.

'Now, Miss. Understand, we're not accusing you of anything, but we think you're withholding information. This business is questionable, very much so. It has a smell,' holding his nose and making a dramatic face.

The little Patricia was not as fragile as she looked, as Raymond had noticed. She had, very likely, the brains of a humming-bird, but she had character. Going to Italy, getting her Jo away from all this, had been her scheme; she wasn't going to give him up easily.

'Information my foot,' she said with spirit.

'How did you come to meet a boy like this, with a very dubious way of living; respectable girl like you?'

'That's nonsense. He's been silly, fooling about on that yacht; I know all about that. But he'd thrown it all up. We were going to Italy to get married; he'll settle down. He's not stupid. It's just here where there's too many people who do no work. This place would corrupt anybody.'

'Yes yes yes,' impatiently. 'That's no defence for making money out of old men on yachts who like boys.'

'He did nothing that's illegal.'

'Now, Miss, I'm not here to discuss morality with you; my job is facts. I want to know when you were both in this town last – and think carefully.'

Patricia decided that, when in doubt, it never does any harm to tell the truth. It couldn't incriminate anyone.

'I can't see what that has to do with it.'

'I'll be the judge of that.'

'I think we were here about a week ago, and then drove over to Sainte-Maxime.'

'Now please tell me in detail where you went, what you did, and whom you met.'

'We just came over for the evening from Cannes. We came to meet a friend who lives in Porquerolles. You see it was quite accidental – just that here is half-way, about, between Cannes and Hyères.' It seemed a good answer. She knew nothing of the last meeting between Jo and Raymond. The only person who knew that was Dominique.

'And who is this friend? What does he do?'

'I don't know. He lives on a boat. He brought it over. We had a few drinks on it. That's all.'

'The three of you?'

'Oh there was a girl there. I don't know her. She works somewhere in a hotel. We just went back to Cannes. Nothing suspect about that, is there?'

'And the name of this friend?'

'Ramon is all I know. He's Danish or German or something. He lives in Porquerolles and that's all I know.'

'And the girl?'

'I only know her as Dominique. Ask Jo if you're all that interested.'

'That'll be all for now.'

He was about to ask Jo, without much hope of getting anywhere, when a coincidence struck him. Porquerolles. This thingummy's wife, the actress – good-looking woman – she had been staying there. The man had mentioned it when he came round. 'Ring up my wife; she's in Porquerolles.' Not any possible connection, was there?

He went to see his superior officer, who listened, drawing aeroplanes with his left hand, shrugged, reached for the telephone.

'Hôtel Suffren? Commissariat of police. Get me Madame Servaz, will you? ... there just might be something in it. Very dubious. Still ...'

'Why I thought I'd tell you, Commissaire.'

'Allo? Madame Servaz? I excuse myself for disturbing you, Madame. Simply that it would help if you could confirm a detail for us. When at Porquerolles, did you or your husband notice or have any contact with a man who lives, it appears, on a boat? All we know of him is that his name is Ramon or something of that nature.'

If – despite me – they succeed in understanding ... thought Natalie. A most malicious stroke of fortune that would be. It would almost look as though I were an accomplice.

'There is a man I've heard called Raymond by the islanders. I've been out fishing with him; he has a sort of yacht. Pleasant fellow. Can that be whoever it is you're thinking of?'

'Sounds probable, Madame, but it's only a confirmatory detail; sorry to have bothered you.'

'Not at all.'

The policeman put the phone down, left his hand a moment lying on the receiver, picked it up again.

'Get me the bureau at Porquerolles ... You're speaking with Cogolin at Saint-Tropez. There's a chap on your island that lives on a boat, not French; name Ramon or Raymond ... You do? What d'you know about him?'

'Know all about him,' came the quiet voice of the Porquerolles police force. 'Yes, lives on a boat – nice little boat – goes sailing, bit of fishing in an amateur way. Does nothing for a living – a bit "gentle-man", you understand. Amiable, friends with everyone, no trouble.'

'What does he live on – or don't you know?'

The voice in Porquerolles chuckled.

'We don't have many secrets here – things get known. He lives on some income – gets a cheque from some bank abroad every couple of months. He supplements it a bit maybe taking tourists for rides, telling them stories perhaps – our local speciality, hm? Haha. Harmless. Very quiet, spends no money.'

'Good. It probably has no importance, but purely as a precaution ... See if you can raise this fellow, would you? Ask a couple of inoffensive questions, right? Make a note and ring me back here. I want to know, first, where he was yesterday evening and last night, secondly, was he at Saint-Tropez about a week ago for the day? And if so, I want the names of the people he met and a brief description of the evening he spent. If he makes a fuss be friendly and reassuring, say that it's simply to confirm details of a story told by someone, no need to worry, etcetera. Got the idea? Right.'

'He'll probably be in the harbour; I'll take a little stroll down there.'

'That's it.'

The Commissaire started shading his aeroplane with neat parallel strokes.

'Let's have this Corsican boy in here; I'll try him with this tale ... Sit down, you. Want a cigarette? Now,' jovially, 'let's get to know a little more about you and your background. Your friends, for example. Tell us about them. To make a start somewhere, tell us about this friend of yours in Porquerolles, Monsieur Raymond.'

'He's just an acquaintance; what more do you want?' The Corse shrugged and injected a sleepy look into the electric-blue eyes.

'Just a little tiny notion I had. Is this one of your financial friends, whom you cultivate in hopes of a bit of pocket-money?'

'I scarcely know him. Why not ask him?'

'Might be an idea. Just asking you first.'

'I've nothing to say.'

'You'd plenty to say about, for instance, Mr Proctor. Can I take it that this is a personal friend? More of a real friend?'

'I don't know what you'd call a real friend. My friends aren't yours, that's for sure.'

151

'How would you define friendship?' still jovial, pleasant. 'Someone you can trust, isn't that it?'

'If you like. I haven't said he was a friend. Just an acquaintance.'

'Come, you know him better than that. He was here in his boat last week; you had dinner together with two girls. Drinks and so on.'

'I don't know what you're trying to get at.'

'Would you call him trustworthy? I'll put it in simple words for you. Would you call him a chap who wouldn't give you away?'

'Give what away?'

'Never mind, it's not important.'

'Am I free to go?'

'Oh penses-tu,' with a laugh. 'I think you're going to get to know us quite well.'

'I don't quite get this, chief,' said the secretary, admiring a second aeroplane that was appearing on the Commissaire's scratch-pad. This one was a pursuit plane, diving on the other, attacking it. 'Do you think there's anything in this?'

'I don't know myself,' indifferently, adding now a little childish dotted line, representing bullets. He pushed it away with a laugh. 'I'm just thinking about the characters of these boys – especially Corsicans. Give nothing away. Loyalty to pals above all else. Now if this fellow with the boat, whoever he is, were totally unimportant, or just a possible touch for a few francs, there wouldn't have been such careful answers, would there? In my experience, they're voluble enough about anything they think a useful red herring. I get the impression that this fellow means something to him. By keeping his trap so tight, it adds to his importance – you get me?'

'You think it might be the source of the information?'

'Why not? We're theorizing, just playing with airy hypotheses, mm? Using what few things we know for sure, we have this boy, here a few days ago, eating and drinking with a chap on a boat. Nobody denies that. Now this boy we've got wouldn't know anything about money in a picture-shop. The other fellow had – we're told – some contact at least with the wife on the island.'

'You think he got a tip and passed it on? But why? What does he gain?'

'Well, if he hasn't much money, and lives a bit on tourists, he might have learned that occasionally one can sell items of information that appear worthless. Little bits of not-quite blackmail, and ... it fits the facts as far as we know them, no?'

The telephone rang; the secretary answered, and passed the receiver across. 'Porquerolles.'

Apologetic voice at the end of the wire.

'Can't get much for you at present, Commissaire. Chap was in Giens for fuel. They say he's left there. Boat's been seen heading out to sea. Gone for a sail, I suppose.'

The Commissaire thought, looking out of his window. The mistral had increased considerably in force over the last half-hour; the palm-trees were huddling and streaming. Saint-Tropez is a bad place for mistral.

'What's the weather like there?'

'Moderate so far, but looks like boiling up for a big one.'

'Seems a queer day to pick for a pleasure sail.'

'I'd think so myself. Water in the Passe is beginning to look angry. Anyone who was out is home by now.'

'Mm. Well, if you see or hear anything, keep in touch. What's this boat like, by the way? Big boat?'

'Hell, no. Sort of converted fishing boat, about twelve metre.'

'Any special features? Can you give me a brief description – I might ring up and see if he's along the coast somewhere.'

'Easy.' The Porquerolles policeman was an islander, and had an eye for a boat; he had even talked to Raymond about it. 'Old-fashioned-looking, and foreign – comes from up north. Square stern, straight bow, deep in the water. Cutter rig.'

'What colour?'

'Black – sails tanned. Deck painted white. Like I say, no flare like our boats – looks real foreign. It stands out.'

'It's enough, or should be. By the way, you've seen Madame Servaz, I suppose – this actress who's been staying with you?'

'Sure. Left this morning in a hurry – auto accident or something with the husband. He was here for the weekend. This chap we've been talking of took her to the mainland – was going anyway to Giens for oil, from what I hear.'

'Did he now? Tell me – they knew each other, then?'

'Ach, I think she was out sailing with him a couple of times.'

'I see. Okay, thanks.'

'Beginning to look as though something were adding up, perhaps?' said the secretary.

'Too vague – just wisps of supposition. It's another tiny point, perhaps, to add. Might as well go on now we're this far.' He still had the phone in his hand. 'This boat must stick out round here like a bowler hat... Miss, get me coastguard headquarters at Toulon... Allo – pass me Monsieur Martin; Commissariat of Police, Saint-Tropez.'

Once in the open sea, Raymond could concentrate on sailing; it did him good. A tussle: *Olivia* was staggering under her mainsail. He reefed it right up and fiddled with the head-sails till she was running more smoothly. Real sailing; never at home in short, hollow seas, *Olivia* tripped and trampled still like a runner among heather. But she was travelling as fast as ever she had done, nearly.

He was out of sight of land, now – a real passage. He felt an exhilaration, as though after interminable hours of groping and stumbling in dark tunnels he had come out at dawn on open moorland, with a wind blowing. He shouted into the wind, feeling bone and muscle in his body, feeling the tiller kick powerfully under his hand. He had not lost everything; he could still handle a boat.

He went and got some whisky to warm himself up, with pride in himself, and pride in the boat, lying easier now, no longer burying her nose or bludgeoning. He stood, and swept the horizon with his glasses. Nothing – a cargo boat far off, plodding towards Marseilles. No small boats – the mistral had frightened them all into harbour. He was alone at sea. He felt pride in being alone, in being a seaman, in being captain of his boat.

*

'Allo Commissaire? Martin here at Toulon. Bit peculiar – this boat of yours exists all right; filled up with oil this morning at Giens, was presumed on the way back to the islands, but now nowhere to be seen. Sounds as though he's headed out to sea. You serious about this?'

'No, not all that much. A very vague theory I was amusing myself with. He'll come back to earth, presumably, in Carqueiranne or somewhere.'

'Sea's getting up – he won't make a port round here. I only mention it because if you really want him signalled, it can be put on the telex, but you won't see a small boat back round here till this blows over.'

'I'll let you know.'

The policeman was considering. Nothing further to be got from Fred, from the old woman, from the shop-manageress, from the railwayman. He had himself been over the building, carefully. Mm, a bold and fairly skilful break-in. Yet it had taken two to climb that wall. And the Corsican was known around here, and had various friends.

But he didn't think much of them. Unpalatable, possibly, but too featherweight. Hangers-about, spineless and mostly penniless livers in tents. Someone had thought this up who had more brains than they did.

The Corse, he thought, had the nerve and the lack of scruple to climb walls and hit people over the head. But the Corse would tell him no more now.

He needed a bit of leverage. He thought of Natalie, but he didn't like the idea much. Well-known actress – might have acquaintances capable of stirring up a wasps' nest if he pushed her too far. Still, it was worth an effort, he decided, balancing advantage and disadvantage of doing anything. If he cleared this business up promptly, it would do him no harm, no harm at all. He put his hat on, and took a little walk over to the hotel.

He had a pleasant moment here. There was a porter who, he knew, had organized a call-girl service. A sly, greedy bastard, but a frightened one.

'Ring Madame Servaz for me, ask if she can spare me a quarter of an hour ... I had a chat with Doctor Potineau this morning – he was giving me some recent figures on venereal disease.' Sweating sneak. 'I can see I'll be ringing up one of these days, inviting you to the bureau for a chat.'

'Always happy to co-operate, Commissaire.' False jauntiness. The policeman leaned familiarly against the porter's desk and gazed around: his eye fell on Dominique, in her chambermaid's uniform, handing a pair of lost-and-found bedroom slippers to the reception clerk.

'That's one of your girls, I rather think. Hm?'

'Madame Servaz asks you to excuse her for five minutes.'

'Very well; I'll wait.'

He cast round for something to do. Why not kill two birds with the same stone? He was here anyway.

'Tell that girl over there to come here; I want a word with her.'

The management wouldn't like his questioning an employee in the public rooms. Well, it would be a useful hint to them to watch their step a little. There had been one or two slightly dubious happenings in this hotel last season.

'I want a word with you, my girl.'

Dominique put on a face of stupid insolence, but though she was by no means bright she had been putting twos together and getting fours. She had heard something about Fred – it had been mentioned among the staff this morning. And when Natalie had turned up, she had understood what had lain behind Raymond's phone-call to her the day before. If she had known that the Corsican sat at that moment in a dingy room in the police bureau she would have been paralysed with terror. But already badly scared she put two more twos together when the Commissaire called her. This time she got five. Something had leaked – something of which she had guilty knowledge.

'You're sleeping with too many men lately, my girl,' began the Commissaire in a sharp nasty voice. 'You get these phone-calls, you go out for little parties in villas and on yachts – you understand me? – and it leads to a prison sentence for proxenetism.'

La bella iocchi didn't know what proxenetism was. The Commissaire had certainly counted on this – he wanted to scare her with a big word.

Oh my god – he knew. That she had spent the night with Raymond – that Raymond had telephoned her. Did he know everything? She felt as though the finger of Jehovah had suddenly come from a pillar of cloud and pinned her flat and grovelling to the stony ground.

Yes – and he was waiting to see the Servaz woman – oh God – what was she to do?

The Commissaire was delighted to see the effect he was producing. Aha, with this one he could drop a hammer on that obnoxious porter. Look at her splendid big stupid eyes – they were huge and blank with sheer terror. He was thinking of how to follow up this unexpectedly easy success when that toad of a porter came sidling up.

'Madame Servaz is in the bar.'

'Give her my compliments and say that I won't be a minute. I'm learning interesting things here,' meaningly.

The porter knew this phrase was for him.

Dominique knew that it was for her.

'Monsieur, I didn't know, I promise I didn't know. They didn't tell me what it was about.'

No need to tell her he had no idea either what it was about, but his eyes bored into her terrifyingly.

'Go on.'

'I only knew he'd met Madame Servaz and he said it was interesting and I had to ring up Cannes straight away. Honest. I swear I know no more than that.'

The policeman had a sensation of several loud brassy fire alarms having been let off very suddenly, just there by the back of his head.

'Stay there. Stay exactly where you are.' He marched to the desk. He hadn't a clue, but he was going to find out, oh yes. 'Call the nearest uniformed agent.' The porter had gone rather green around the gills, and scurried out.

A salute. 'At your service, Monsieur le Commissaire.'

'I want you to take this girl here to the bureau, and tell Inspector Barthou my instructions are she's to see nobody till I come. Right?'

'Sir ... all right, Miss. Come on; no need to bother about a coat.'

The bella iocchi's long beautiful legs were shooed through the revolving door. The Commissaire stood trying to collect his thoughts for a long moment. He had an impressive frown, but he had forgotten all about the organizer of call-girls. He walked slowly towards the bar.

'Please forgive me, Madame – unavoidable delay – a word with what may prove a vital witness. What can I offer you? Two whiskies with ice, barman... To your health and your husband's speedy recovery. And, if I may add, to my own speedy tying-up of this disgraceful affair.'

'I feel sure of that,' said Natalie politely.

'I wanted to ask you, Madame – you see, this all undoubtedly hangs on some piece of information that proved incomplete. Someone knew your husband possessed a fairly large sum of money, and yet did not know that he would leave on Sunday night and call at Saint-Tropez on his way to Paris. Now did everybody in Porquerolles – it is a small place – know when your husband was going?'

This needs some care, she thought. My answer can easily be checked.

'I don't think anybody knew. He had intended to leave on Monday, but suddenly decided to go earlier and save time. But what difference can it make?'

'Simply checking on the source of the information the breakers-in undoubtedly possessed. We will have to talk to a few people in Porquerolles. Your personal affairs, of course, are no concern of ours – but for instance, this chap, the one who lives on the boat – it appears that it was him who brought you over this morning, to the mainland?'

'Oh yes, that's so. I was thinking of going fishing, and was actually on his boat when the message arrived. Very kindly he offered to take me across. I demurred, but it seemed he had to go anyway – some question of having to get petrol or something.'

'I see. What is puzzling me is that this man certainly went to get his petrol, but did not return to Porquerolles. Vanished you might almost say. We are interested – somewhat – only because he has friends we suspect might have been concerned in this affair. He didn't by any chance mention that he planned to go somewhere?'

'No, but there was as far as I know no reason why he should. It was coincidental. I was there, I got a hasty, possibly garbled message brought by a fisherman, and I was preoccupied with getting to the mainland quickly. I was worried, you see – I thought there had been a motor accident and that my husband was dangerously hurt.'

'Yes of course, I can quite see how you would have reacted. Just one last query, Madame, if you will forgive me. It is not aimed personally. Did you at any time, while on holiday, form an impression that this man had any interest in you or your husband's activities?'

Natalie laughed and drank off her whisky.

'An island acquaintanceship. You know how they are. One is short of company, and thrown into that of various picturesque strangers. This man seemed to be of some education and to have travelled widely. I certainly found him agreeable, and passed pleasant hours listening to his island tales. You know these island tales. Picturesque but exaggerated. Island gossip – essential ingredients of the Porquerolles bouillabaisse.'

He laughed.

'Yes yes, indeed, quite so. It's of little importance.'

'I suppose he might just have gone for a sail. I recall his going off for a couple of days while I was on the island.'

'Seems a bit sudden – and in a mistral?'

'Men are sudden – look at my husband.'

'Yes yes, haha. Well. Many thanks, Madame, and I'm sure I'll have no call to trouble you further.'

'Don't bother about that. Quite at your service.'

I hope, she thought, that I have been adroit.

Chapter Sixteen

Back in his office, the Commissaire had leisure to consider his windfall.

'Barthou, you talked to this little English girl that was picked up with the Corse. What was it she said again – they'd had an evening here on the boat and there'd been some other girl, who'd stayed on the boat after they left – wasn't that it, roughly?'

'That's right. Some girl called Dominique.'

'Ha. I believe – I admit by pure chance – that I've put my finger on the exact girl.'

'Not the one you sent over . . .?'

'Exactly. Bring her in . . . Your name, I believe, is Dominique . . . good. Admirable. Sit down, my dear, have a cigarette. And now – if you'd be so kind . . .'

Dominique, who had absorbed the tenets of the Corsican, wanted to lie to the police. But she had been knocked off her balance, and could not recover it. How much did they know? Just now, when she had hardened herself to telling them nothing, they'd suddenly confronted her with Patricia. Seeing her meant just one thing: they'd got Jo.

If she told the truth, she reasoned, she might have a better chance of being believed when she told them she had no idea of what had been planned or what had gone on.

The Commissaire, listening with a kind face to a hasty gabble about scooters and phone-calls and the Café du Phare, could recognize the truth when he saw it. He was quite satisfied, especially when, with an adroit swerve, he was able to rope in that porter on a charge of proxenetism. After twenty minutes, he was able to reconstruct the entire movement between Giens and Cannes on Sunday evening. He called the inspector.

'I think we might as well let the two calves go. The English one knows nothing at all, and the other, the one with the eyes – I could have her for concealing criminal knowledge, but I used her to screw that call-girl lark. You can pull in that porter. Now we've got the Corse – just this other bird.'

The secretary had waited till his boss was finished with the girl friends, but he had news too.

'Toulon rang up. Their spotter helicopter's seen the boat. Out at sea – a few kilometres south of La Ciotat is the reported position, heading roughly south-west into open sea. Monsieur Martin thought you might be interested.'

'I am, very. Get him for me on the phone.' He lit a cigar, a thing he only did when in a good mood. He had been clever. But he wasn't denying having been very lucky too. He was most grateful to the bella iocchi.

'Toulon for you.'

'Hallo Monsieur Martin. Here, Cogolin. Very many thanks. Tell me, twenty odd kilometres off La Ciotat – farther by now presumably – that's not international waters or anything? It's your territory still? ... I know, but with material evidence ... robbery with armed assault, my brave; I think that's quite enough, don't you? ... Tell me, this helicopter of yours can arrest people, huh?'

'Too true it can,' Monsieur Martin was saying in Toulon. 'Frequently does. Not in these circumstances, perhaps. Lot of mistral, and it's whipped up a naughty sea. Might be tricky putting it on the water ... Armed assault, eh? Might he have a gun, this johnny? ... Well, I've a patrol-boat off Sanary – I can get it over there ... Qué, catch him? Our boats can do forty knots. I'll have him for you in Toulon this evening.'

'Fine, my popote. I'll buy you the apéritif next time I'm in Toulon. Say hallo to your wife for me.'

The Commissaire busied himself with this and that, and was agreeably surprised to see quite soon that it was time to think about an evening drink. It had been a good day; he would go home in a beneficent frame of mind, and perhaps take his wife to see Belmondo in the new gangster picture. He put his hat on to cross the road to his car, and was only slightly ruffled when a violent gust of mistral blew it off and he had to chase it, with three tiny street-urchins applauding.

'Hoi, hoi, holà, it's the Commissaire. Holà, Colonel.' They imitated the sound of police sirens, whistles, and machine-guns, with great verve. He made a good-humoured feint at kicking the nearest bottom and climbed cheerfully into his car, towards home and pastis and vegetable soup.

Raymond had wished to go farther south, but with the mistral at full force by now the hollow waves were too much for *Olivia*'s square flat transom. He had had to turn increasingly towards the west, and he had even so to settle to the hardest job a steersman has: keeping a small sailing yacht going in a sea that is too big for her.

Olivia was a good sea-boat, but built as she was for the long unbroken Atlantic swells she tended to trip and crash through waves where she should have ridden smoothly up them. Green water, solid and wicked, shipped over her bows too often. Raymond did not mind the lash of spray in his face but this was dangerous; he had to surrender finally. He turned her into the wind, lashed the tiller to keep her sheered, and took the mainsail off altogether. Immediately she lay to calmly, with a motion still short and uneasy, but not dangerous. No longer any risk of swamping. He pumped a fair amount of water out of the bilge, wondering a little uneasily whether it had all arrived over the top, and whether some was not seeping through the patched hull.

But he was happy. Not for a long while had he had the sheer content of hard sailing off a heavy wind. He was not scared of mistral. It was not like the gusts of an Atlantic north-westerly, that strips a boat's sails off her, bows her with irresistible force to her waterway, burying her gunwale, and may dismast her, sending her drifting helpless to a death that may be slow. This was only mistral, and he had known worse ones at that.

Nor, strangely, was he eaten with fear for the hull. This sea was strong enough, arriving with smashing hammer-blows, to tear the rotted planks like wet newspaper. He had not even the precarious safety of the dinghy, still moored in Porquerolles harbour, dipping and nodding at his abandoned anchors. Not that it would help him much if he had. One cannot tow a dinghy in a sea-way: it is a great drag and, worse, it feints and veers. One must get it on deck – upside-down on the cabin roof. And if *Olivia* did sink, she might sink so quickly that there would be no time. And if there were – he might not survive long in a dinghy in this sea, not single-handed, with nothing but a pair of oars. No, he did not regret the dinghy.

He was not even frightened; he no longer cared. A freedom had come to him. However accidentally, feebly, unpreparedly, he was on his way. A way that would eventually lead him across the South Atlantic, around the dreadful cape, up the icy iron coast of Chile, to the sweet mimosa climate, and the beautiful hills and bay of Valparaiso. He had shaken off Europe, and with it twenty years of humiliation. Whether he had left in deliberate calm or in a feeble tantrum mattered not at all. He was sailing.

He went below and had something to eat, made sure everything was tidily stowed and secured, checked the pump. No more water than there should be. *Olivia* was lying comfortably head to wind and drifting a mile or two an hour. He could have slowed this rate but preferred not to. The drift was off shore.

Back on deck the sea looked less formidable, and the tearing whine of the wind in the wire rigging was even reassuring. He picked up his binoculars. Nothing to see at all, anywhere, now. An open sea, uncontaminated. He would take a star-sight at nightfall, but he knew that he must be off Cap Sicié still, not even as far as Marseilles yet. A westerly course led him across the gulf, which would be bad if a storm blew up; he must get farther to the south. But on his course he had made twenty-five miles odd, and another hundred and twenty would see him off the Spanish border by Perpignan, and that was country he knew.

He had no fatigue, no misery or pain. No hunger or thirst troubled him. He was very nearly perfectly happy.

He had no thought for Natalie, or the police. He had left suddenly, but none of his movements were suspicious or even questionable. He had a right to cut the bonds that had held him tied and crippled, glued helplessly to the comfortable lazy islands.

Suddenly, he felt his whole force concentrated on this voyage. He had for so long wished that it could be so. And, to achieve that, he had paid a heavy price. So be it. Now, nothing would stop him. Nothing.

His coffee had gone cold; he poured some whisky in and put the lot in a flask. That would be a fortification tonight against a long spell of steering. He stood up and laughed, looking forward to it. From joy, and the release from a sticky bird-limed snare in which he had for too long flapped helpless wings.

At that moment, he heard the helicopter.

He knew it, ugly thrashing whirling thing, nosing and spying over the coast, though he hadn't thought it ever came this far out to sea. Looking for suspected carriers of contraband – this wasn't the forest-fire season yet. Well, he was carrying no contraband. It passed him low overhead and he waved at it cheekily, flippantly, as he had waved once from the same deck to Natalie. It came back then and hung over him, making an appalling noise. That irritated him, to have this monstrous dragon-fly brooding over him, and what could it see in him anyway? He and his boat were well known along the coast. He was relieved when it went. As the noise of the motor was drowned at last by wind he thought that, anyway, would be the last token of the life he had left behind.

A vague unease pestered him, all the same. He was not yet far enough from the land; he hadn't yet quite detached himself; a sticky thread or two still clung.

He looked at his watch. Nearly five; he was surprised to realize that he had been nearly seven hours at sea. He would try to put a few more miles behind him; time enough at dark to heave to if the wind strengthened. Had the mistral dropped a little? Perhaps it was only a one-day blow – they went, classically, in multiples of three after that. He would sail some more.

He ran forward to set the jib; *Olivia* bucked sharply and the quick pitching movement increased his impatience to be gone from a world where there were still craning, peering eyes. He cast loose the rope that held the sail brailed up, scrambled back to the cockpit, and turned his boat off the wind. She surged forward at once, firm, resistant, nothing slack or weak about her. Under head-sails alone she sailed well; it was like having a horse under him. He cuddled the wriggling, kicking tiller well into him and ducked happily as the first bucketful of spray came flying over into his screwed-up eyes.

The wind might have slackened a little, but the sea was even higher now, he thought. He was bullying *Olivia* a little, throwing unnecessary strain on her, asking too much. Well, he was asking it of himself as well. He could not stop. He could not put too much distance between him and a land where everyone was hostile, had hidden sarcastic smiles as they bade him good morning, had never understood. He would be contented, now, only when he was in mid-Atlantic, on the old sailing route, far from these bled-out, worn-down people, smeared with dirt and grease and money and hypocrisy, from greedy women and men like Fred, that thought with money with their little mean adding machines. Well, he had sloshed him. He could not even feel remorse for it – not yet.

The commander of the patrol-boat that at five that afternoon was idling back from the direction of Sanary towards Toulon and home was a man who had developed a thoroughly professional grip upon his job. He kept his personal feelings behind a hard impassivity. He was a most experienced officer, a little old for his job, which he was very good at. When arresting suspect boats at sea, he gave one clear warning, and closed in fast, before anybody had time to throw things overboard, or look at him along sights, let alone be evasive. He always made thoroughly, professionally certain; he kept a gun trained on them. He had been shot at many times, and had once had a hand-grenade tossed on his deck.

He had been trained in the heyday of the smuggling out of Tangier and Spanish Morocco, the years just after the war when anything fetched a good price in France. He had been hardened over the years by the gun-running to the Algerian rebels. That had been a business that had disillusioned him very greatly.

Being still only the commander of an armoured preventive launch had made him a little sour and harsh. He had little humour. But there was no one like him at hearing the faint beat of a far-off motor at night, at choosing the right angle of approach, at coming alongside a boat at speed, when a fraction of a degree in the angle can crush two hulls like eggs. As a ship-handler, as an eye behind binoculars, as a plotter on a chart or estimator of a strange boat's speed, he was swift, sure, and deadly. But at understanding anybody at all, from Algerians to his coxswain, he was no great shakes. He had recently been divorced from his wife, for being too free with a fancy girl in La Seyne. This had not improved his nature or sweetened his tongue.

The patrol-boat was a fast, lean ninety-footer, perhaps narrower and deeper than a torpedo-boat, which at speed planes over the surface. But she was scarcely less fast, and more manoeuvrable. She had little armament considered as a war boat, though a good deal considered as a coastguard. She had very powerful lamps and a big machine-gun. She had surface radar as well as ordinary direction-finders, and she could talk to ships, shore or aircraft by radio telephone. Her speed and striking power, her commander's cunning and shoot-first mentality, made her a terror to every would-be contrabander within fifty miles of Toulon.

It took no great effort to find Raymond; the mistral and the sea had brought 'grass' on the radar, but there was still daylight, visibility was excellent, and the helicopter had plotted a rough position. By seven the reddish-tanned sails had shown up to the eyes on the patrol-boat like a glass of whisky to an alcoholic.

Raymond did not notice the thing sliding up at a loose, comfortable half-speed behind him. He was concentrating utterly on the sea. Sometimes coaxing, talking to himself, sometimes singing gaily as a bucket of spray stung his right ear, sometimes hardening his jaw muscles and pushing his lip out as he luffed to a steeper sea, and *Olivia* tossed her nose and went over like a steeplechaser. Leg over leg, the little dog went to Dover. When he came to a stile – Hop, he went over.

He had found his touch, the steersman's instinct, knowing

exactly how much pressure to give the tiller to keep his boat running sweetly. And when suddenly the loudhailer crackled at him he reacted as Octavian does to Ochs. Who is this personage, loud-mouthed and coarse, with his vulgar jokes and his disgusting familiarity?

From first to last he never thought of the police. He had, these last hours, forgotten Fred, forgotten Natalie. They might have been the happiest hours since his early childhood. Not even the first night he had slept on board *Olivia*, after buying her, had he quite lost the sense of the world pressing in on him. There had been other times, sailing, when he had known something of the same absorption. But then there had been cold, hunger, always fear. Dread of not making his landfall, fear of what the sea and the wind could do to mast or rudder, of darkness, of rocky coasts to leeward. There had always been ominous reminders.

Now, fear had left him. For the first time, there was absolutely nothing to be frightened of.

And now this fool, shouting at him distracting him, breaking his concentration. A three-ha'penny customs man, having no doubt nothing better to do. What did they think they were playing at? He waved his arm upwards in an irritable dismissive jerk, watching the sea, not even looking at them.

'Keep off,' he muttered. He turned his head a second, on a crest, and shouted it. 'Keep off.' They couldn't hear him, of course, to windward, but he wasn't interested anyway. 'Drown yourselves.'

Damn the fellow, he knew him. Had drunk at the same bar half a dozen times in Porquerolles. 'He knows me perfectly too; hasn't he got the sense to open his eyes and recognize me?' he muttered angrily.

'Heave your boat to,' called the quartermaster through the loudhailer in his trained sharp voice. He lowered it, watched the figure in the cockpit of the little boat, slightly astonished. Fellow didn't even raise his eyes; first time he could remember seeing that.

'Does not respond to the order, sir,' superfluously. The officer was standing right beside him, and could see as well as he did.

Certainly the captain of the boat knew Raymond. Had seen and spoken to him in Porquerolles. Thought him a thin poor thing. No bone. He was slightly indignant that this fellow, who had apparently committed some crime, had now the insolence to disregard a plain order.

When a French patrol-boat calls on you to stop – you stop. Don't ever think they're joking.

'Thinks we're fooling,' said the officer indifferently. The patrol-boat was idling at dead slow ahead. Without her great power – two hundred and fifty horses – to knife her through the seas, she pitched, irritatingly.

'Or doesn't understand French,' suggested the quarter-master. Foreigners . . .

'He does. But since he pretends not to, we'll speak a language he does. Half ahead. Give him a word across the nose there, at two hundred metres.'

When she forged ahead with a jump Raymond, glancing from the corner of his eye, thought only that he had, belatedly, been recognized. They must be asleep.

'Attention,' spoke the machine-gun suddenly. Often in a train, as one sits gazing out of the window, lulled by speed and movement, another train passes, an inch as it seems from one's nose, with a sudden shriek. Machine-gun bullets, fired just ahead of one, have something like the same sound and effect. Even at sea, with the water fighting you, and the wind of a mistral humming in your ears and the rigging, you are startled.

But not frightened. Raymond was not frightened. He was extremely angry. So much so that if he had had a gun he would have fired back.

'Trigger-happy bastards. Call you to stop as though you were a bloody dog, and if you don't, fire off a machine-gun at you. All they know. All they're bloody fit for. Peasants.' He had to luff, suddenly, to a big wave and jerked his mind sharply back to the sea. He wasn't going to heave to, not for an aircraft carrier, let alone that thing with its delusions of grandeur.

It disconcerted them when Raymond paid no attention. The purpose of the gun was to make him obey, and he did not obey. He should have been very frightened. But one is not frightened by the passing train either. It is on a different line. It does not hit one. If it did, it wouldn't make that slightly unnerving sound. You don't, they say, hear the one that hits you.

Had there been less sea, the commander might have risked putting his boat alongside. But in a seaway, even if it is very calm, boats cannot approach one another without great caution. The faintest touch, barely perceptible, will destroy a boat, though landsmen, even after the *Titanic* and the *Andrea Doria*, do not know this.

The patrol-boat commander knew that a boat the size of *Olivia* could break him like an old lamp bulb. With both boats tossing and heaving to an angry sea, *Olivia* would have to be put head to wind, and then kept quiet and obedient while he approached gingerly, with two seamen on the foredeck holding rope fenders. Raymond did not obey, nor did the machine-gun make him. Yet the commander of the patrol-boat was not an old woman crossing the road, scared both to go on and to come back. He turned his boat in a sweep, flashed past at barely fifty yards, and gave Raymond a dose in the hull with the machine-gun as he passed. That, he thought, would teach him to stay still when told, and the exercise of collecting Raymond's body could then proceed as planned.

What happened was not what he had intended. The double handful of bullets that was all that were fired hit *Olivia*, rising at that instant to a wave, just on her exposed waterline, pierced right through her – at that range they would have pierced planks double the thickness. She plunged on into the trough of the next wave, which hit heavily straight on the patch just aft of the bullet-holes. The rotten wood and the pierced metal sheathing gave way altogether. The effect was of the whole midships section on both sides being torn straight out. A fourteen-inch shell could not have done its work better.

Olivia, driving on into the next wave, disappeared as did Uncle Abishai. She did not even leave a few floating remnants behind. Raymond went straight down with her. His grave cannot have been so far after all from Master Gunner Peyrol's.

Natalie kept her counsel and was never bothered by any

169

more policemen. Fred got his picture from the old woman in Saint-Cloud and his money from the insurers. As for the Corse, he got clean away with it. He was nearly six weeks in jail, but they never managed to prove anything conclusively, and out of loyalty to his dead comrade he never tried to put the blame on Raymond. Dominique, who thought she had been the instrument of sending Raymond to his death, decided to become a nurse; she made quite a good one.

Six months and more afterwards, Natalie was reading *Lord Jim* for the first time. She had forgotten her own words, and did not recognize them when she saw them, but she was struck by Stein's famous remark: 'One must oneself in the destructive element immerse', but even more by the weighty words of the pompous, gloomy mate, Mr Jones, whose acuity so struck Marlow: 'Neither you nor I, sir, had ever thought so much of ourselves.'

Well, Raymond had himself in the element immersed, hadn't he? Thoroughly, for good. Perhaps in that way he had got to Valparaiso after all.

More about Penguins

Penguinews, which appears every month, contains details of all the new books issued by Penguins as they are published. From time to time it is supplemented by *Penguins in Print*, which is a complete list of all books published by Penguins which are in print. (There are well over three thousand of these.)

A specimen copy of *Penguinews* will be sent to you free on request, and you can become a subscriber for the price of the postage. For a year's issues (including the complete lists) please send 30p if you live in the United Kingdom, or 60p if you live elsewhere. Just write to Dept EP, Penguin Books Ltd, Harmondsworth, Middlesex, enclosing a cheque or postal order, and your name will be added to the mailing list.

Some more Penguin Crime is described on the following pages.

Note: *Penguinews* and *Penguins in Print* are not available in the U.S.A. or Canada

Edmund Crispin

Gervase Fen, Oxford Professor of English Language and
Literature, claims to be 'the only literary critic turned
detective in the whole of fiction'. The genial eccentric could
also claim to have placed Edmund Crispin, with Dorothy
Sayers and Michael Innes, on the recommended reading list
for bishops, judges, and cabinet ministers, present and future.

The Moving Toyshop

The toyshop in the Iffley Road contains the strangled body of
a grey-haired woman when a friend of Fen's enters it one
night. The next morning the toyshop has vanished and a busy
grocer's store occupies the site. And nobody's surprised.

It's like investigating a crime that hasn't happened. That
suits Fen.

The Case of the Gilded Fly

In *The Case of the Gilded Fly* the corpse of Yseut Haskell,
an attractive bitch of an actress, is deposited almost at the
door of his college rooms. She has been shot in the head.
Now anyone who knew her *would* have shot her: but only one
man *could*.

And Fen knew who that was within three minutes.

Not for sale in the U.S.A.

Ellery Queen

Face to Face

Ninety-one books and 100,000,000 copies after Frederic
Dannay and Manfred B. Lee became Ellery Queen, the great
investigator solves an astonishing New York murder mystery.

Glory Guilde (née Gloria Guldenstein), middle-aged chanteuse
married to much-wed 'Count' Armando, scrawls 'f a c e' on a
pad in her penthouse as she lies dying from bullet wounds.
Ellery Queen is called in, with Harry Burke (from Interpol),
a straightlaced Scot who falls for a nubile witness.
Sophisticated, flip, mordantly funny, set in elegance and
sleaziness, *Face to Face* confounds until the last chapter.

Cop Out

Malone is a loner and a good cop – until hoodlums take his
daughter as insurance for a stolen payroll and a murder.
Then he is just a father. And he's scared.

But there's a way to get her back – possibly at the price of
his career. Almost gone too far to be a cop again, he takes one
last desperate gamble . . .

Also available

The New Adventures of Ellery Queen

The Origin of Evil

The Player on the Other Side

Ten Days' Wonder

There Was an Old Woman

Not for sale in the U.S.A. or Canada

Nicolas Freeling

Double Barrel

They told Inspector Van der Valk to pose as a bureaucrat, go to the dreariest town in Northern Holland and forget he was a policeman. They wanted him and his wife to become small-town eavesdroppers and 'peeping Toms' like everybody else. Just to find out who was writing letters so poisonous that two people committed suicide and everyone was scared of everyone else.

It could have been Van der Valk's dreariest job . . . except that he found out a lot about himself, and his wife, small towns, and just by chance uncovered the worst unpunished war criminal since Eichmann.

Criminal Conversation

Van der Valk always got the cases no one else would touch. The ones that would have been better hushed up. Rich people, powerful people with friends in high and low places should be handled with kid gloves. But Van der Valk wanted to know all their nasty secrets . . . why a sixteen-year-old girl and her mother were so involved with a rich society doctor . . . why a drunken painter who knew too much dies so conveniently of natural causes . . .

Also available

Gun Before Butter

Love in Amsterdam

Not for sale in the U.S.A.

Nicolas Freeling

Tsing-Boum

Esther Marx, the wife of a dull Dutch sergeant, is killed in a dusty, dreary district. Machine-gunned during a TV gangster serial full of bangs to cover the noise. Leaving behind a daughter of doubtful parentage . . .

As Commissaire Van der Valk investigates, he finds strange links between this municipal murder and events in Dien Bien Phu in 1935: Esther had been more than a camp follower; dusty files, old soldiers, and old scandals slowly surface to form a puzzling pattern of cowardice, blackmail, jealousy, and revenge . . .

This is the Castle

The writer Dutheil, famous, difficult, a recluse, is drawn more and more into the violent country of his imagination.

Does he in fact live in a castle with valuable antique furniture? Is he having an affair with his secretary? What really does the American journalist want in coming to interview him? And what about his feelings towards his daughter – incestuous or disciplinary?

The crunch comes at the end of a long, tense day: does he kill?

Not for sale in the U.S.A.